Hers

by

Paul Dutton

For Caroline.

And for Jennifer, Edward and Christopher…

Three more Stars in the Universe.

Chapter 1.

'We're all going to Herstmonceux tomorrow, Ceux tomorrow, Ceux tomorrow,

'We're all going to Herstmonceux tomorrow, we can stay all day,

'We're going to the Ceux, Ceux, Ceux,

'You can come too, too, too,

'We're going to the Ceux, Ceux, Ceux,

'We can stay all day.'

So sang the young astronomers before they moved from Greenwich to Herstmonceux. They sang it in the pub on leaving night which he said was a cross between a celebration and a wake. I didn't understand what he meant by that, just as I didn't know what the word 'irrevocable' meant when he used it with a smile to describe their relocation.

I've learned a lot since then.

He'd be proud of me.

{ I was.}

Chapter 2.

It was difficult to concentrate in lessons on the north facing side of the school.

The teachers there were convinced it was their fault so for a while they gave me the benefit of their doubt and I was encouraged to participate more. Questions in class were increasingly directed towards me and when it was time to read out a prepared answer I knew who was going to be the first to be asked. I tried to prime a corner of my mind to listen out and be ready to respond but even that soon became distracted and the teachers lost patience. They let me know it too. Eventually exasperation became worry and they consulted with the teachers from the south side of the school.

'He's fine for us.'

'Yes, no problem at all. Good as he ever was.'

'Which lesson was this? Geography? Well what do you expect!'

The northsiders withdrew, hurt.

A letter arrived home. It was addressed to my parents and signed by the headmaster which made it a very big deal indeed. I had no warning and the first I knew was when the letterbox opened and snapped shut again depositing the letter on the carpet. Shandy, our golden retriever, barked and ran towards the door. In an ideal world she would have eaten the letter but I had trained her not to do things like that so it sat there until my Mother picked it up and placed it in front of my Father. He glanced up from his newspaper.

'Bit early for your school report, it must be all of a fortnight before you break up for Christmas.'

'How do you know it's from David's school dear?' asked my Mother.

Dad grinned, 'I recognise the typewriter. It hasn't changed since I was there. Look. The full stops come out only half printed and the 'S' in 'Smith' is smudged.'

'Very clever dear.'

Dad looked taken aback.

'Careful observation. That way you get fewer surprises,' he muttered, pulling open the envelope. He read the single sheet of paper which was enclosed and his eyebrows shot up. So much for fewer surprises. His eyebrows returned to normal and I could see him thinking furiously.

'Erm... David.'

My hand, holding a piece of buttered toast aimed at my mouth, stopped halfway and I gulped.

'Yes Dad?'

He tried to frame the question so that it didn't shock me or Mum too much and he put on a conversational tone as if receiving bad news from school was the most natural thing in the world.

'It says here that you're ahh... slipping behind a bit in some of your lessons... err... and that one or two of your teachers are a little worried about things and erm... wondered if there was anything wrong that you aren't telling us...'

His voice trailed off and he held the page up to the light examining carefully the head's signature in case it was a forgery.

'No... no... Everything looks ok here.'

But Mum had heard.

'What do you mean ok? It doesn't sound as if everything's ok!'

Dad put the letter down. 'No, you misunderstand, I mean the signature. I recognise it.'

'Let me see that!'

Whatever plans Dad had for softening the blow disappeared. Mum read the letter at speed. First came the explosion:

'What on Earth is this! We've never had anything like it before!'

Then the accusation:

'What have you been up to?'

Third was self-reproachment:

'It's my fault. I should have kept my eye on you but I thought you were growing up and could be trusted to get on with your schoolwork without me constantly checking.'

Fourth was reflection:

'But you must have been or we'd have heard about it sooner. So this is recent.'

And finally the dénouement: She looked at me with a steely gaze.

'I think you have some explaining to do young man.'

I developed a stammer.

She waited.

My stammer became worse. Dad also waited. I found it hard to look at either of them. Perhaps time would come to my rescue, before long I would have to leave.

My Mother realised this.

'I can see this is causing you some difficulty. We'll resume this conversation later and maybe then you'll be able to explain yourself.'

I ran out of the door and on the way wondered what difference eight hours would make? There would still be the same question and I would still have no reasonable answer. What could I say then that I found so difficult to say now? How could I describe the excitement of what I could see out of the window directly north from school and how much more thrilling it was than lessons. My imagination was captured completely and there was none left for schoolwork.

Golden Hemispheres were burning bright in the cool Sussex countryside.

{We only had David's best interests at heart.}

Chapter 3.

'This is it, Professor,' shouted Matthew-Day, the youngest astronomer and therefore the last to have joined the Greenwich observatory.

And therefore the one with the fewest regrets about leaving, mused the Professor, his tidy mind neatly filing the thought in its correct place. Times had changed. He wondered how long his own career would have lasted if, forty years ago, he had dared to address his own Professor in such a carefree manner.

'Are you sure you've got everything!'

The Professor raised his eyes to heaven.

Matt Day heaved his rucksack onto the ex-military truck which the civil service had provided. Professor Maclachlan picked up his briefcase from where he had placed it at his feet. Not for him the back of a lorry, seniority still had some privilege. A rather battered Bentley awaited along with an equally battered ancient chauffeur who touched his cap and invited the Professor into the rear of the vehicle. Miles Maclachlan hesitated. Seniority had other privileges too; he had spent the best years of his life at Greenwich and if he had to leave he would be the last to do so. He held his briefcase tightly and looked back.

The final army truck roared off.

'Are you ready Sir?' asked the chauffeur.

It was hard to leave.

'Strange to think I'll never see this place working again,' the Professor said quietly, 'I suppose they'll turn it into a museum.'

'What was that? My hearing isn't what it used to be, could you speak up?'

Miles Maclachlan smiled. Many things weren't what they used to be.

'I'm sorry, I apologize. Yes, I'm ready to go.'

That seemed to satisfy the chauffeur who waited until the Professor was settled into his seat before closing the rear door firmly. He walked slowly back around the car giving his passenger more time to look out of the window at the abandoned observatory. Finally, he took his place behind the wheel and adjusted the rear-view mirror. For an instant the Professor was reflected, his head turned away, still looking back.

The chauffeur finished his adjustments and started the car engine.

'They've taken the 'A' road,' he said.

'Pardon?' Professor Maclachlan was still lost in his memories.

'I mean they've taken the obvious route Sir.'

'No doubt because it's the fastest?' The Professor was in no mood for conversation. This was one time he wanted to be alone with his thoughts.

'That's what they think. How would you like to beat them?'

The Professor finally looked away.

'You mean you know a quicker route?'

'Local knowledge Sir.'

When the convoy finally arrived at Herstmonceux, the Professor was idly leaning against the Bentley looking at his watch and when he was sure he had been seen he walked over to the final truck in line. Matthew Day couldn't contain himself.

'How did you get here before us?'

'FTL Travel Matthew, Faster Than Light. I discovered it last week. I had meant to tell you.'

'No, really, please tell me how you did it?'

His face looked so earnest that the chauffeur coughed to hide a laugh. 'Will that be all Sir?'

'Yes, thank you,' replied the Professor, 'It was a very pleasant journey.'

The chauffeur touched his cap and before he left said, 'I hope you don't take too long to settle in here, it looks as though they've gone out of their way to make you feel at home.'

'I'm sure we'll be fine,' agreed the Professor, 'Thank you again.'

The Bentley drove off and a sudden silence descended on the group. The Professor let it go on for a moment. He had visited this place several times whilst planning the final move so the surroundings were not new to him. Most of the others hadn't and now they were realising there was no going back. The drivers of the army vehicles were unloading bags and suitcases and dumping them in the courtyard without making any attempt at sorting them out. They behaved as if they were in a hurry to leave and didn't mind who knew it. Soon they were finished and ready to go. They too had caps but they didn't touch them and they didn't wish anyone luck settling in before they left. They reported to their Captain who in turn reported to Professor Maclachlan: 'All done Sir, we've checked all of the vehicles, they're empty.'

He saluted but obviously didn't expect the Professor to return it because he immediately spun on his heel and shouted for the convoy to leave. With a roar of engines they departed.

The silence in the group had gone on for long enough thought the Professor. They were here now and had better make the best of it.

'All of you, gather your things and follow me, the accommodation block is this way.'

It must have been the effect of being around the military for even a short time. He sounded too much like a sergeant-major and that was not the impression he wanted to give.

{I never had to be much of a leader, at Greenwich the group more or less ran itself with just the lightest of touches necessary to keep things moving smoothly. But relocating to Herstmonceux required a different approach, one with which I was never entirely comfortable. Many of the old guard had not come with us, they had taken the opportunity to retire; I found it hard to blame them, we really were completely uprooted from the life we had known. The younger astronomers of course found it all a great adventure, particularly Matthew, and while I admired their enthusiasm I recognised that they would need firm guidance especially in the early days. I'm not sure I achieved the correct balance between leading them and ordering them around but I only had the example of my wartime experience to fall back on. Perhaps things would have been easier had I modelled my style more on the wise senior officer I hoped I would be against the bossy RSM I am afraid I became. But you only get one chance to do anything which is important – and hindsight is, of course, the clearest vision of all.}

Chapter 4.

The astronomers realised what an effect their arrival would have on the locals and issued invitations so people could see for themselves what was happening at Herstmonceux. The school received one. A group of pupils (not too large) could visit and have a guided tour followed by lunch. And if their behaviour was suitable the same group would also be able to visit at night and actually use one of the telescopes to look out into the Universe.

The teachers argued for a while about who to send but couldn't agree so they announced a competition, the winners of which would form the lucky few. The competition was to research the history of the observatory at Greenwich and give a presentation to be judged by the headmaster. It was announced at assembly and caused a terrific fuss. I looked at the northside teachers. They didn't want me to win. The southsiders did, they hoped it would help get the whole thing out of my system. I stared at the northsiders and hated them.

'One book in the whole library.' Philip Teston sat on his own looking over to a table at the far end of the room where a set of six of our classmates poured excitedly over a leather-bound reference book, taking notes on pads. 'We're next, I've spoken to the librarian.'

Phil was my best friend in school and we were entering the contest together. 'How long have they had it?'

'Fifteen minutes. Everyone gets the same time, I've asked.'

I thought about this. 'With just the one book?'

'That's right.' Phil hadn't stopped staring at them. Now I noticed that under the edge of our table, where he thought no-one else could see, Phil held a stopwatch. His eyes flicked down toward it then back up again. 'Two minutes and twenty seconds.'

‘Phil…’ I began. There was a commotion in the distance followed by much scribbling.

‘They must have found something exciting. Damn.’ He glanced down again, ‘One minute and fifty-five seconds to go.’

‘Phil,’ I said more urgently.

‘What?’

For the first time he stopped observing either the other table or his stopwatch and paid attention to me. I knew Phil and I knew I didn’t have long to make my point before he became distracted again.

‘Well, it’s this.’ I tried not to sound impatient. ‘What are we going to find in that one book that six of them haven’t?’

Phil continued his countdown but I could see my words were hitting home. ‘One minute and thirty seconds...’

‘Look, you’ve done well getting us next in the queue…’

The librarian must have also been timing because she rose from her seat. She looked at us then started to move slowly towards them.

‘When it’s the only thing you’ve got you have to use it,’ said Phil quietly, ‘You know that as well as I do.’

I didn’t say anything in reply. My sentence before last was corrosive enough.

The librarian’s clock inside her head kept perfect time because she didn’t interrupt them immediately but paused on her way and looked back at us raising an eyebrow. Did we still want her to intervene?

Phil didn’t meet her gaze, instead he muttered something under his breath, pressed the reset button on his stopwatch, and slipped it into his pocket. She didn’t notice and when her count reached zero she walked over to the far table and retrieved the book. She brought it to us and sat down again in her seat.

‘We’re wasting our time here,’ I urged Phil. He wouldn’t look at me either.

‘We can still win,’ I added, ‘We just have to find another way.’

The book remained on our table unopened. We went, and the librarian looked hurt as she watched us leave .

{We couldn’t just let him go, not after the way he had treated us and our lessons. Things got no better after we persuaded the Head to send a letter home to his parents, he still wouldn’t pay attention and he looked out of the window all the time at that observatory and its blasted domes wishing no doubt that he was there and not with us. It would just look like giving in and we knew he knew it. If he actually won the competition then fair enough…}

{I was hurt.}

Chapter 5.

It was a bus journey to the library in the nearest big town and we made it after school. It didn't close until six so that gave us an hour. Anything to delay me having to explain myself to Mum.

We didn't get the bus often, Phil and I, the last time had been just before Christmas a year ago when we needed to be alone to buy presents for our families. Now it was just before Christmas again but presents would have to wait, we had more important things on our minds.

'It's not fair giving us only until tomorrow to do this,' Phil said.

I disagreed. 'It's a test of our resourcefulness,' I told him, 'Who else will think of doing what we're doing?' We both looked around at our fellow passengers while pretending not to. Pupils from the school were with us of course, this was normal, it was the usual way for them to return home. But we listened to what they were saying and they weren't talking about the competition, libraries or the observatory. In fact, their conversations were boring. We breathed sighs of relief. The other passengers were old people and obviously they were no threat. The bus took us past the new buildings but the view was disappointing and nowhere near as good as the one from the north side of the school. Something had changed though, as we found out when the bus slowed suddenly when we weren't expecting it.

'It's a temporary stop,' I told Phil as I looked out of the window.

'Right outside the observatory gates,' he said. 'Swap places, let me see.'

'No.'

'Let me!'

'You can see on the way back,' I said.

'I won't be able to, I'll be on the wrong side!'

He was right, but I wasn't going to move. The bus ground its engine noisily into low gear. Why was it stopping anyway? Surely there must be someone waiting if a bus was to halt at a temporary stop. Someone to request that it did. But we had been concentrating too much on outside. From behind us a figure rose and made his way to the front. As he went past I saw he had blond hair and wore a heavy coat but he moved too quickly for me to see his face. The bus came to rest.

'Thank you,' I heard the blond man say clearly to the bus driver. 'I don't know my way around yet so I wouldn't have known it was here I had to get off. Well spotted!'

'That's alright, I'm still getting used to it myself, it will be a permanent stop soon but I know it now so you'll have a gentler ride next time.' The man was getting off. He must work here. He must be an astronomer.

Well, thanks again.' The man paused. 'Er… Have I worked this out correctly? You drive this bus in a circle, I mean, it was you who took me into town that way,' he pointed at the road ahead, 'And now it's you bringing me back but from the other direction.' The driver smiled.

'You're all educated men, I expect you could work something like that out in your sleep.' The blond haired man grinned. 'I dread to think how far I'd have to walk if I'd missed this stop.'

Phil nudged me. 'Four miles is the answer.'

'A long way,' said the bus driver.

'Well, thanks again.'

And with that the blond haired man got off. The bus pulled away.

'I know exactly how far it is,' Phil said. I didn't doubt it. Phil was good at knowing things like that. I watched the man but he didn't turn around. Then the bus took a corner and I lost sight of him.

It was raining when we arrived. We ran to the library and got wet dashing fifty yards from the bus-stop. Once inside we concentrated on not panting and when we succeeded Phil and I approached the front desk.

'Yes,' whispered the librarian, looking at us as disapprovingly as the school version had.

'We're sorry about the noise, we've been running,' explained Phil.

'It's raining outside,' I added.

'Have you no umbrella?' she whispered fiercely.

'It wasn't raining when we started out,' said Phil, dropping his voice level to match hers and looking around. 'We didn't mean to disturb anyone.'

'Just because it wasn't raining then is no reason for you not to plan ahead. This is England after all.'

We looked at each-other. Neither of us knew how to respond to that. Phil tried apologising again.

She looked at our uniforms. 'Your clothes are wet. What will your Mothers think?'

I groaned inwardly. I was already in enough trouble, now I could add ruining my uniform to the list. If I got wet again on the way home I resolved to wait until my clothes dried before I faced Mum. But it was no good, the woman must have been a mind-reader.

'And don't think you can just let your uniform dry on you,' she said looking straight at me, 'Your blazer will shrink and so will your shirt!'

A counter started up in my head. It gave the percentage chance I was going to ask the librarian how she could possibly know what I was thinking. She knew all right. 'Twenty percent' said the counter, Forty percent, Fifty percent...'

I couldn't help myself, I was going to say it.

'Seventy percent; Seventy-Five...'

I was saved by Phil.

'Excuse me but we are looking for books on astronomy, we want anything you've got on the Royal Observatory, the one which was at Greenwich in London but which has now moved to here, well near here anyway, its moved to Herstmonceux.' That could well have been the longest speech Phil had made in his life.

The lady behind the desk looked startled for a second then composed herself. 'Word gets around quickly,' she informed Phil. My percentage counter reset itself to zero.

'They've been building it for months, we can see it from school,' Phil said, enthusiastically.

'I wasn't talking about that.' She eyed Phil, 'I was talking about what happened an hour ago. One of your astronomers was here.' Phil's eyes grew wide but I put it together quickly.

'He had blond hair didn't he?'

'Oh, so you know him?'

If only we did. Regretfully I shook my head.

'Well then.' She looked satisfied she had regained the initiative.

'Why was he here?' asked Phil.

She looked at us, one to the other for a long moment and then something seemed to give and she stopped trying to obstruct us. She reached behind her desk. 'This is why. He said he was on a goodwill mission.' She held up a book. 'He said he had been told to drop it off at the nearest library and say it was a gift. He would be happy if we would place it on our shelves. He said they wanted people to know the history of the observatory.'

This was fantastic news. The book was exactly what we were looking for.

'Can we borrow it, I mean not take it out of the library but just look at it, me and Phil?' All my words came out together in a rush.

'It's not on the shelves,' said the librarian slowly as if reminding herself, 'And I haven't had time to give it a card yet so technically…'

Even Phil knew when someone old wanted to do something for you but just needed that final push. 'Please,' he said. And smiled.

'I really shouldn't, it hasn't got a ticket and you could just walk out of here taking it with you…'

But she had reached the top of her hill of indecision and Phil's smile had pushed her over it.

'…So long as you stay where I can see you I can let you have it until the library closes.' She smiled back at us and though she really tried her smile wasn't pretty.

We took the book to a table and opened it. We both made notes and on the bus back we learned them.

When we returned home it had stopped raining and my clothes were mostly dry. Mum did resume her conversation with me but to my surprise it wasn't as bad as I thought it was going to be.

{'You're all educated men'. I liked that! I wonder if he would still be impressed had he known there were men who couldn't be trusted to tie their own shoelaces working at the observatory! Probably. Even they knew enough to pass their paper qualifications around at such moments and it usually did the trick.

I hope my errand delivering the History of the Observatory at Greenwich did some good, I didn't mind going, it wasn't as if we were allowed out much anyway because there always seemed to be something else to do back at our new site. I loved exploring new places, I just didn't get much time to do it with the hours we had to keep. Our surroundings were certainly different. I wonder when we'll be allowed to go out for a drink? Not before Mother Goose Maclachlan has checked out the pubs himself no doubt. I wish he'd get on with it. I'm sure he thinks of himself as our fearless and dauntless leader but it's really not him. Even I, who have been part of the group for the shortest time, can see that. He is trying though, which is sweet.

I wonder if those boys up ahead are coming to see us? I wonder if anyone will? I wonder if we're really as interesting around here as we think we are? So far all I've heard is that the villagers have complained about the colour of the domes.

No, it will be the youngsters who are interested. They'll be the ones bitten by the bug. And if its anything like it was for me when the bug bites it will bite hard.}

{I thought carefully what to say. I didn't want to go overboard again, I'd already done that with my tactic of the five stages of displeasure. I think David got the message. Nothing like this had ever happened before, a letter from his School was unknown unless it contained his report (invariably good up to now) or an invitation to parents' evening (invariably bad according to David's Father as it meant the headmaster would lean on him for a contribution to the School Fund). I wasn't that concerned if the truth be known. It was surely a temporary blip which would soon right itself. I decided not to play the harsh card again. It was too soon. After all, David was a boy and boys were supposed to have a rebellious streak weren't they?}

Chapter 6.

Each class in our year had its own contest before morning break. Who won would be decided by the form teacher and the winner would go through to the overall final to be held in the school hall. It would be all over and the result known before lunch. Phil and I spent the morning break on our own telling each other we must have won the preliminary round and must therefore go through.

The end of break bell sounded. Our year didn't go to normal lessons but instead filed into the hall. The teachers who had listened to us sat grouped around the Head at the front of the stage. When everyone was quiet the headmaster announced that the class winners would now make their presentation. I wondered how it was decided who would go first.

We weren't the ones to start.

We weren't second either, or third. Phil sunk his shoulders down and moved lower in his chair.

When we weren't fourth his head dropped and he wouldn't even whisper to me never mind talk normally. He was being an idiot and I told him so. That earned me a glare from the nearest member of staff standing at the side of the hall. I sat waiting for the group on the stage to finish speaking. They were taking ages.

We weren't fifth either. Phil looked like he had given up.

At last they finished. 'Now, the final contestants. Applause please for…' I knew it, they had saved the best till last.

Phil was on his feet before I was. One thing I knew was that if you were any good it didn't matter whether you were speaking in front of three, thirty or three hundred. I didn't know if Phil knew that so I tried to send the thought to him, silently. If it was received nothing showed. Loud applause accompanied our walk to the stage. Later on some of those who clapped so loudly told us it was because they were happy it was going to be the last time they would have to sit and listen to exactly the same thing. Because we didn't know that it spurred us on.

Phil started at the very beginning.

'The Royal Greenwich Observatory was ordered by King Charles II in 1675 and at the same time the King created the position of Astronomer Royal who was to be the Director of the Observatory'.

I gave the Astronomer Royal's duties: 'To Apply Himself with the most Exact Care and Diligence to the Rectifying of the Tables of the Motions of the Heavens and the Places of the Fixed Stars so as to find out the so much Desired Longitude of Places for the Perfecting of the Art of Navigation.'

Phil set the scene: 'In 1675 Greenwich was a village in open countryside several miles outside London. But London grew and swallowed the village. Smoke from factories and houses and the discharge from mercury vapour street lights destroyed the 'seeing'. But Greenwich was famous. The Observatory had to move but the name couldn't be lost'.

I took up the story: 'Why not go to a mountain top? Why choose Herstmonceux, close to sea-level and prone to mists?' Here I paused. The book had been no help, all it said on the subject was that there had been 'extensive investigations' before the location of the move had been agreed. But the extensive investigators had got it right, despite the mists the location did provide more clear nights than anywhere else in England.

Phil described the extensive plantations which had been made, to reduce atmospheric turbulence and to shield the new buildings housing the telescopes from the sight of the dismayed locals who objected to them spoiling their view.

Then I played our trump card. Tucked away in the back of the book we had found a few pages ripped from the 'Architectural Review' of the previous year. The domes housing the telescopes were made of copper and if anything seemed deliberately designed to provoke the locals they were. No-one had so far mentioned why copper was chosen. The ripped pages made it clear. Over time, copper would turn green as it oxidised and then the domes would blend in with the countryside. Out of the corner of my eye I saw my chemistry teacher nod with satisfaction. I concluded: 'The domes might look odd now but soon the local people will see that the designers were in sympathy with them'.

We hit our stride: Greenwich was the provider of the 'pips' which were broadcast by the BBC to signify Greenwich Mean Time. Astrophysics had been invented there when observations on positional astronomy had led to investigations into the nature of stars and galaxies. The Ministry of Defence's Chronometer Department, responsible for the servicing and repair of naval chronometers and RAF navigator's watches was attached to the observatory.

And then there were the telescopes themselves.

We didn't understand anything of how they were constructed or how they were operated and of course we hadn't seen them but the names were enough. I remember the names to this day and how they caught in my imagination:

The Thompson 30 inch Reflector;

The Yapp 36 inch Reflector;

The Great Equatorial 28 inch Refractor;

And one that was planned for the future: The 100 inch Isaac Newton Telescope. This was going to allow Britain to compete with the giant telescopes already constructed in America and Russia.

We knew we went on for too long but I knew we were going to win. Phil and I would actually see these things next week as a guest of one of the astronomers at Herstmonceux, perhaps even the blond haired man we had seen yesterday.

It was over. We returned to our seats in the hall. The teachers gathered around the headmaster in a huddle at the back of the stage and deliberated as we talked excitedly to each-other. Finally the head stepped forward and made his announcement.

We hadn't won.

{I suppose I did allow myself to be talked into it but I stand by the decision as firmly as if it were my own. You see, although the standard was high there was one obvious winner but that's not all there is to leading a School. I know Philip Teston and David Smith would disagree with me because they, being pupils, see things in absolute terms but when they mature – 'grow-up' I suppose they would disparagingly call it – they will realise that given their behaviour in school I really didn't have any choice. My first job, it may surprise them to know, is not to ensure fair-play but to keep my staff happy. A happy staff makes for a happy school. Yes, it will contain disgruntled individuals as a result but that is a price well worth paying. As they grow older Teston and Smith will find themselves using the same principle in their everyday and professional lives and I hope then that they will recognise the difficult position they placed me in. I think I can be certain about that. It was John Stuart Mill who put it best...}

{We won. You heard the announcement. We're going to see it before you. We're going to see it all.}

Chapter 7.

Professor Maclachlan took a deep breath and walked into the local pub.

He wasn't a drinker and he wasn't noted for seeking out the company of strangers but this visit was part of his job. The new buildings had caused a stir in the village and he knew enough to realise that his astronomers had the potential to do the same unless the situation was handled carefully. Accommodation was at a premium at their new site and Nissen huts were all very well but couldn't cope with the sudden influx of personnel. Some senior staff could afford to buy a house nearby but for junior staff just starting their careers it was a different story. It was up to him to break the ice.

'Good evening Sir,' the barman greeted him, 'What will it be?'

'A pint of best bitter.'

The barman pulled it and as he did so looked over the new arrival. 'Just passing through are you Sir?'

'No,' answered the Professor, 'I'm part of the group which has moved here from Greenwich. I'm sorry but this is the first chance I've had to introduce myself. My name's Maclachlan, Miles Maclachlan.'

The barman placed the pint of bitter on the bar towel and offered his still wet hand to the Professor. 'Well, there's a coincidence. My name's Miles as well, Miles Crowner. Nice to meet you.'

The Professor took his hand without hesitation. Strange, he thought to himself, how it's so often the little things which work in ones' favour. 'Thank you. This is a lovely part of the world, very different to South London.'

'Oh, we like to think so.' Miles the barman laughed and Miles the Professor joined him.

'You're the first of the New Strangers who's ventured this far, you're not going to tell me you'll be the last?'

Professor Maclachlan heard the capital letters very clearly. It was inevitable such a label would be given and until they became known as individuals the tag would remain. To begin the process of its removal was also part of his job.

'No, I doubt I'll be the last.'

'We'll look forward to seeing them here then. You don't mind your staff having a pint?'

'No, they're human like everyone else. You have to remember of course that their working day is the other way around, most people would enjoy a pint after they finish work but in our case that would be around five in the morning and I don't suspect you'd be open then.'

The barman stared at the Professor. That was something he hadn't thought of. 'We do have the occasional after hours,' he said, 'But nothing like that…'

'I'll pass that information on,' said the Professor nodding gravely and waiting. The reaction wasn't long in coming.

Miles the barman burst out laughing. 'Don't tell me you came here just to check I wasn't open until dawn!'

'No, you're right, there is something else.' The Professor stopped smiling and took a sip of bitter. 'I was hoping you would be able to help me with something.'

'Me personally?'

'Maybe, or through the people you know in the village. Perhaps both.'

Miles the barman raised an eyebrow. Perhaps he was about to be asked to provide a crate of beer on a daily basis so the astronomers could take it away and keep it until it was required when the sun came up. He speculated briefly about how they would keep the bottles cool, did they have a fridge up there as well as their telescopes? Then the thought occurred that they wouldn't need a fridge, they could simply leave the crate out of doors, the cold night air would do the rest. What else could it be? He shook his head.

'I give up. You seem to have everything you need up there if the gossip is to be believed.'

It's now or never, thought Professor Maclachlan. If this didn't work plan B involved crossing the road and putting a card in the post-office window. Not ideal. He stayed optimistic.

'The thing is, we've moved here at rather short notice and I am desperately in need of accommodation for my younger staff. They'd have to be housed close to the observatory so they could walk to and from their work. I couldn't rely on public transport at the odd hours they arrive and depart so that means accommodation here in the village. I wondered if you knew of anyone who'd be willing to take them in. It wouldn't be forever.' The Professor paused. 'I'm happy to guarantee they'll be no trouble,' he added hopefully.

'Well.'

Miles the barman hadn't imagined he would be asked that. He picked up a clean glass and started to polish it.

'Well.'

The Professor waited.

'I'm surprised you don't have accommodation for your people up there already considering your work must be important,' he said.

'National importance,' agreed Professor Maclachlan cautiously, 'But you know what Whitehall is like. There isn't an awful lot of money around – but there's enough to pay a decent rent,' he added hurriedly.

'Well now.'

This isn't going to work thought the Professor, he's hedging too much.

'Well now,' said Miles the barman, suddenly brightening, 'I can't help you myself I'm afraid but I don't see why others couldn't. I don't know everybody's exact circumstances but I'm sure you'll find some will be able to oblige, especially if you put it to them as you've just put it to me.'

'Can you give me any names?'

'I think you'll be better asking directly. People respond to that better, what do you think?'

'I'm happy to take your advice but who is it I should ask?'

The barman smiled. 'Are you in a hurry?'

The Professor shook his head.

'Then have another pint and we'll see who comes in. It's early. In half an hour I guarantee you'll have some luck or I'll stand you your next.'

The Professor sighed inwardly. Aside from himself the pub was empty and trade looked slow so this might merely be a way to increase it. On the other hand he couldn't just walk out. He placed his empty glass back on the bar and looked at the full one which immediately replaced it. For someone who didn't drink he could get a taste for this. 'Cheers,' he said, raising the fresh glass to his lips. Oh well. There were worse ways to spend a damp December evening in the week before Christmas.

{'He seems like a down to Earth bloke for an astronomer. Likes a pint so can't be all bad.

Interesting it's his youngsters he's looking to place in the village. I must tell Mrs. Miller, she'll take one of 'em in if she's got room, which she will have when she gets fed up of her latest lodger, haw!! And when she finds out its work of national importance involved she'll throw herself into the job; do anything to help she'll say, I can hear her now.

I hope whoever she gets has plenty of stamina, he'll already have been up half the night and if what I've heard is right he'll have to be up all day as well if you catch my drift. Mr. Miller won't complain though, he never does.

He's looking a lot less knackered since she started taking in. When he comes for a pint he actually stays awake these days instead of putting his head in that bowl of nuts over there and nodding off. So everybody wins, that's the way to look at this, haw haw haw…}

Chapter 8.

Phil and I had talked about it as much as we wanted to. The inquest had been conducted furtively in lessons and loudly in between and at the end of it we had each decided one thing which the other refused to accept.

Phil: Ok, we lost. Now we just have to get on with it.

Me: The northside teachers had got their revenge but if they thought I was now going to work in their lessons they were wrong. Doubly wrong because I would redouble my efforts to not work. They weren't going to beat me.

Phil pointed out the logical inconsistencies in my stance then shook his head at me and walked off when I refused to bend.

When I arrived home I went up to my room and carefully sorted out my homework into the pile I would do and the pile I wouldn't. I did maths before tea, keeping a baleful eye on the other pile. Before I went downstairs I pushed my geography book to the bottom of it and left it there.

As usual after tea Dad took Shandy's lead from the wall and slipped it around her collar.

I put my coat on.

I usually went with Dad during the summer when it was warm so this was unusual and Dad asked me why I wanted to come now. I couldn't tell him the real reason, which was I had plenty of extra time now I wasn't going to do my geography homework, so I said I wanted some fresh air. He looked at Mum. Neither of them said anything so we left.

I wasn't allowed inside the pub so I took up my usual summer place at a table outside and tied Shandy's lead around one of its legs. Nothing changed as far as we were concerned. Dad reappeared immediately from the pub with a bowl of water for Shandy and a glass of lemonade for me. Then he went back inside.

I sat at the table and sipped the lemonade. Tomorrow the winners of the contest would visit Herstmonceux. The contest Phil and I should have won. They would see the telescopes and if their behaviour was good they would be invited back to look through one. I hoped they misbehaved. I hoped they brought disgrace to the school and wrecked a telescope costing the school thousands of pounds. The repair bill could be taken from the money the teachers got paid. That would show them. Then they'd have a bad Christmas and it would serve them right. They'd have to sell their cars or something. But only the northside teachers, I reminded myself.

Shandy barked and I looked up to see why.

Walking toward us were a man and a girl.

They were walking slowly and the man was looking around himself all the time. This told me he wasn't from around here or he wouldn't have found every single thing so interesting. He was talking to the girl all the while but she had been listening to him for too long because she wasn't even pretending to be interested. She wasn't talking. When she noticed me she smiled and looked up at the sky. Then the man saw me and Shandy.

'Sonja, this is a Pub!' He seemed delighted. 'A Country Pub! I must go in. Look, here is a boy about your age, you can practice your English speaking with him and you can make friends with his dog. Wait here, I will not be too long.'

He hadn't asked me whether I wanted to talk to the girl who I supposed was his daughter. He didn't know how to leave anyone outside a pub either because he didn't immediately reappear with a glass of lemonade for her. I didn't say anything so Shandy did my job for me and lifted her head so she could be petted. The girl stroked her. I looked at my glass. It was still half full so I could also be friendly.

'Would you like some of this?'

The girl stopped stroking Shandy. 'Thank you, you are very kind.'

'Is that your Dad you're with?'

'Yes, that's right.'

I had to tell her. 'He's not very good with pubs is he? My Dad's inside but he brought a lemonade out for me and some water for her.'

'He's excited,' she said. 'He forgets about me. It happens.' She shrugged and I thought her eyes might go to heaven again but they didn't, they stayed looking into mine. They were the palest blue I had ever seen. 'Karl thinks I need to practice talking English much more than I need to. I speak it better than him but he'll never admit it. My name is Sonja, what's yours?'

'David,' I told her. 'I thought Karl was your Dad, he looks too old to be your brother…and I'm sorry if I've said anything out of place.' I said the last bit in a hurry.

She looked at me and her pale blue eyes sparkled. 'That's alright, you haven't. Karl is my Dad but I stopped calling him that after I was fourteen.'

'Doesn't he mind?'

'He's getting used to it.'

Sonja looked up at the dark clouds above us. 'Does it always rain in England? As it's so close to Christmas I thought it would snow.'

'Only on Christmas cards,' I told her, 'It might snow in January or February.'

'Then I'll miss it. We have to go home before then.' She looked sad but whether it was the thought of missing the snow or the thought of going home I couldn't tell.

'I've never been away from home.'

'I have, many times. Karl has to bring me with him because my Mother died when I was small and there's no-one to look after me. He said he'd find me a place at a school here so I didn't miss any of my education but he hasn't done it yet. Perhaps that's why he's being so long in the pub, he might be organising it now.'

I doubted that but I did so privately. In my experience pubs weren't for those sorts of things but as a foreigner Sonja couldn't be expected to know that. Our village was a strange place to choose for a holiday though, there wasn't much to do unless you went to the south coast and that was deserted in winter, surely she would be better off in London? Maybe they couldn't afford it. Where was she from anyway? I tried to think of a polite way of asking all this but I didn't need to. Suddenly she said:

'Karl is a visiting speaker in the conference at the observatory. He's well known in Sweden; he says after he speaks here he will be well known everywhere.'

She just came right out with it. I was sipping what remained of my lemonade and I nearly choked. Her Father was a famous astronomer. He was speaking at the most famous observatory in the world. He was inside the pub with my Dad right now and I was making friends with his daughter. And she called him Karl.

'You live at the observatory?' I gasped.

'That's correct.' She looked at me strangely. 'Are you all right? You sound out of breath.'

'Just some lemonade which went down the wrong way.' I cleared my throat and gave her a winning grin. 'I'm fine.'

She nodded. 'You make it sound as if it's quite something to be living at the observatory. Well it isn't, it's boring. I have to go to bed at nine and Karl says it's three or four hours after that when the atmosphere around here settles down enough so they can use the telescopes. They do that until dawn then he goes to bed. I miss it all of course. When I wake up I go and wake him up and he sits there drinking coffee and not saying much to me until around twelve when he wakes up properly.'

'You have to expect that,' I told her, roughly, 'Don't you realise your Father is making discoveries, incredible discoveries. They're what he's going to talk about and what will make him famous. You should be proud of him!'

My words didn't seem to matter much. Sonja merely yawned and patted Shandy on the head. 'You don't know him,' she said. 'If you did you'd know he exaggerates. He's done it before.'

Shandy nuzzled her and she responded, stroking the side of Shandy's head. I couldn't believe it. Surely this was jealousy. What could she understand of her Father's work? Then the door of the pub opened and my own Father came towards us.

'You'll never guess what David,' he said while nodding at Sonja, 'There's a Professor in there, a real live Professor! And he wants our help.'

'I know,' I said, 'This is his daughter, her name's Sonja.'

Dad stopped in his tracks. He stared at Sonja for a second. 'Strange,' he said, 'He didn't mention her…'

'Karl forgets to,' said Sonja.

'Karl,' repeated my Dad. 'No, no… This Professor's name is Miles, I'm sure of it.'

'Two Professors,' giggled Sonja.

Dad looked at her as if she was mad. 'I don't know anything about that… Anyway,'

He recovered himself. 'The Professor I met wants somewhere for an astronomer to stay for a while, an astronomer who works at the new observatory.' He looked at me expecting me to be excited at the news. I was but I was trying to not let it show in front of Sonja.

'So I said yes, we could take him in. We have a spare room, he could use that. I'd have to speak with your Mother of course…' Dad looked at me for support. I smiled back. He took that as good sign.

'All being well he'll move in tomorrow… That will make up for you not winning your school contest won't it? I'm sure if we make him feel welcome he'll take you up there with him to visit sometime soon. That's what you want isn't it?'

Why do parents have to say the most embarrassing thing possible? My smile became fixed on my face. Sonja frowned.

'You could have asked me,' she said. 'Why didn't you say?'

'That's great Dad,' I blurted out, 'Thanks. By the way, Sonja wants to go to school here as soon as possible.' It was the first thing which came into my head and I only said it to deflect her attention away from me. She looked surprised. So did Dad.

'Really? Things certainly are getting interesting around here. It's very close to the Christmas holiday so your Father should contact the girls' school this week, with a little luck they'll agree to take you on next term. Tell him that.' He smiled at Sonja but Sonja shook her head.

'We'll have gone back by then. We're only staying until the new year.'

'Ah.' Dad folded his arms and thought for a minute.

'I have it! You be ready in the morning. I'll ring the headmaster of David's school early tomorrow and get you a week's invite to sit in on lessons there. I know him well, he's very progressive about that sort of thing and he won't refuse I'm sure.'

Sonja looked sideways at me. 'Thank you… I think.'

Dad looked enormously pleased with himself. 'Two birds with the one stone,' he announced, 'Me.'

He started on the walk back home. I untied Shandy and followed him leaving Sonja waiting for Karl. At the top of the hill I looked back and she was still sitting there, still without a lemonade.

{A Pub!! I knew there would be one, in every English village there is a pub, it is the heartbeat of the place, I must go in. And there is a boy for Sonja to talk to and keep her company, I have been boring her but she is too polite to tell me so directly, perhaps it is better I should leave her for a moment to make a friend on her own. Yes, that is the correct thing to do. She will be fine – and there is a dog – she likes dogs –she can make friends with it also. I won't stay inside too long, or maybe that is wrong, I should give her time to talk to this boy and to stroke his pet, they will get on well I'm sure of it. Sonja likes talking, she will talk the hind leg off this boy, as they say here.}

{At last someone my own age. I can't decide from looking at him if he is happy or not. His dog is happy to see me because she wags her tail. Some things are common in every language. I give him a sign which says 'grown-ups are awful'. It doesn't fail. Karl disappears and I am left alone with the boy to make the most of it. That doesn't bother me. Karl is insensitive and he always will be, that is him. I am used to making the most of it and that is me. I sit down beside this boy and pet his dog. That, as I knew it would be, was all the encouragement he needed.}

Chapter 9.

My alarm clock didn't go off at half-past seven so I didn't wake up.

Instead, at twenty-five to eight Mum came into my room and pulled open the curtains. As I awoke she put a finger to her lips and whispered: 'No unnecessary noise. Use the bathroom then come down to breakfast quietly. We have a guest.'

I dressed very quickly all the time feeling more and more nervous. In the bathroom every single insignificant noise was magnified until to me it sounded like bells clanging against each-other. Brushing my teeth was a herd of elephants crashing around the room and the door squeaked like a thousand mice when I opened it to let myself out. The stairs on the way to the hall… well, you get the picture.

Mum jumped as I entered the kitchen. 'Goodness me, don't creep up on people like that.'

'I was being quiet.'

'Then I must tell you to be quiet more often. I had no idea you could do it.' She wasn't whispering, she was speaking normally.

'Won't you wake the guest up,' I half-whispered, caught between trying to talk normally and adapting to the Special Circumstances.

'No. He's up in the spare room and that's two floors away.'

'Oh.'

I knew she was waiting for me to ask who it was in the spare room.

'Do you want two slices of toast or three?'

Now I was sure. She had never asked me this before, I always had two slices. It was probably only a friend of Dad's who couldn't make it home and had called in to stay after I had gone to bed. Or maybe there wasn't anyone up there at all and she was just playing a trick on me. Dad came into the kitchen.

'Any sign of Matt?'

That settled it. The Matt I knew worked with Dad. I banged my spoon around in my cup of tea noisily to show them I'd not been taken in. Matt would be downstairs soon because Dad had to leave for work shortly.

'No,' said Mum, 'Matt the astronomer is still fast asleep. David has been most considerate keeping as quiet as possible.'

If I had been nervous in the bathroom it was nothing compared to how I felt now. Butterflies flew around my stomach. 'I thought you were having me on,' I whispered fiercely.

Dad looked puzzled. 'But I did say he would be arriving today.'

'I thought you meant…'

Mum put my plate of toast in front of me. 'I'd have thought you of all people would have known the hours they keep as you're so interested in the observatory.'

'Yes,' agreed Dad, 'They're nocturnal up there. We were waiting for him when he finished work at five am. I still had time for a good couple of hours in bed.'

Dad started to munch his toast. I had a thousand questions I needed to ask but Mum was having none of it. My usual leaving time had arrived and she shooed me out of the door talking all the time. 'Have you got your books? Good. Now try not to upset your teachers. Say hello to Philip for me. Bye…'

I found myself outside my house as if I had been dumped there. The curtains to the spare room were pulled shut. Behind them slept an astronomer dreaming who knew what sort of dreams. On the walk to school I wondered what he had discovered last night.

I was nervous for a different reason during registration but nothing out of the ordinary happened. Phil asked me why I kept looking at the door so to change the subject I told him what had happened last night and about the mystery man who was still asleep upstairs at my house.

'When do you think he'll wake up?' Phil asked.

I made a quick calculation. 'If he got to sleep at five and needs the normal eight hours he should be awake by one in the afternoon.'

'Just in time for lunch,' said Phil, impressed. 'I often feel like sleeping that long. I have once or twice, have you?' He didn't wait for me to answer but carried on: 'Both times I've had the most vivid dreams, everybody is supposed to dream every single night but I can't remember anything about them when I'm forced to wake up but if I'm allowed to sleep I always remember them and in detail. Towards the end I can even direct them. I know I'm dreaming but it doesn't matter. I can make the dream turn out as I want.'

I was half listening and half looking at the door.

'I think people should be allowed to sleep for as long as they like.'

He then went on to describe one of his dreams and I continued to half listen. It was some nonsense about him flying somewhere. The bell sounded before he had finished.

Geography was our first lesson, on the north side of the school. The copper domes were visible glinting through the window. They were closed now it was daylight. What wonders had been seen when they were open last night? I sat with my head turned at a ninety degree angle gazing at them, dreaming my own dreams.

'Today is a special day,' announced Mr. Lewis, the geography teacher. 'The group who won the astronomy contest is to visit the observatory today as part of their prize. Would that group please stand.' Four boys stood up, very pleased with themselves. 'Now make your way to the school reception where you will shortly be met by the astronomer who is to be your guide for today.'

I ignored them. They left. The lesson started and I ignored that too.

'It's Cities,' said Phil, nudging me hard, 'Cities of the World. You were supposed to find out where they are for homework last night.'

'Oh, that's what it was,' I answered.

'Yes, and now we have to write their names in the correct location on this map.' A blank map of the world had been placed in front of us.

'We each have to fill in the names and put our initials by them so he knows who was closest. It's another contest.' There was a long list on the desk between us. 'We've only got ten minutes.'

I looked at the first name on the list. Rangoon. Hmm...

I turned back to the observatory. Walking up to it right now were four undeserving so-called winners. Phil and I should have been doing that instead of them.

Phil dragged my attention away. 'Come on. I've done the first one, now you do it so I can cross it off the list.'

I barely looked where I scrawled the name. Phil almost choked. 'The capital of Burma isn't there, it's not noted for penguins!' I ignored his protests.

'Right,' he sighed, 'Mombasa.' I repeated my disinterested stab at the map.

Phil closed his eyes. 'It's Mombasa, not Manchester.'

That drew the attention of Mr. Lewis who started to move closer.

'Here, I'll give you one,' said Phil urgently, 'Barcelona, that's easy.' He wrote the name in the correct place and put DS after it. Then, not too far away, he wrote it again and added his own initials.

'I saw that,' said Mr. Lewis, making us both jump. 'Let David try the next one on his own. If he doesn't get it right I shall suspect he hasn't done his homework.'

Phil passed the pen to me and whispered 'Good luck.'

I paid close attention to the list. Getting this wrong would mean a punishment and probably another letter home. And if that happened for a second time the result could be costly. My Christmas might be affected. I looked intently at the list. Uppsala. Phil groaned.

Uppsala? Where was that?

'Say it David, it might help you remember,' said Mr. Lewis, his voice hissing like a snake.

At the far end of the room the classroom door had opened but I hadn't noticed and neither had anyone else in the class, they were looking at me hoping I'd get it wrong so they could have some entertainment.

'Uppsala,' I said out loud, followed by, 'It sounds Scandinavian but I'm not sure where, Sweden, Norway, Finland…' I went through the countries I knew hoping Phil would give me a sign when I hit upon the correct one but he was being observed too closely.

'…Denmark, Iceland, Greenland…' I continued my hopeless quest.

'Greenland isn't part of Scandinavia,' proclaimed Mr. Lewis, 'You sound like you're fishing and I suspect you haven't completed your homework. Very well, I'll put you out of your misery. Uppsala is of course…'

'…In Sweden, about one-third of the way up on the left hand side,' came a clear, confident voice from the classroom door. Every head swung towards it. 'I was born there.'

'Well done Sonja,' said the Headmaster who stood beside her smiling. 'And Mr. Lewis, I'm sure you'll allow, what shall we call it, an assist, from such a pretty resident of that fine town. It's usually boys who are heroes in sticky situations isn't it? How pleasant to be part of an occasion where the reverse is true.'

I picked up the pen and wrote Uppsala on the map of Sweden one-third of the way up on the left hand side and followed it with 'DS'.

'Uppsala Sir,' I informed Mr. Lewis and held the page up.

The class collapsed in laughter. Only Mr. Lewis didn't see the funny side of it but he was from the northside and hated me already so it didn't matter.

{He who lives by the sword!! I know Mr. Lewis won't mind being upstaged like that but I might have a word with his class, discreetly of course, if I detect there is any long-term reduction in his authority as a result of this. I'm sure there won't be, the boys know where the line is and they won't cross it.

David Smith involved again I see. He's making quite a name for himself, only a week ago he was an obscure boy in the scheme of things. I'll check all this doesn't go to his head - he seems quite happy now being the centre of attention but he's not really cut out for it, not one of life's natural leaders you might say. When this blows over he'll be back as he was – Nature Will Out and all that.

Sonja will bring him even more fame, in the short term. No doubt she will get him invited to the observatory and with his thirst slaked we can all return to normal.

Sonja. She doesn't look out of place in our school. I suppose I'll be called too liberal for my own good letting her stay but I look forward to a time when girls will naturally be in classes with boys. Perhaps they'll civilise them. But I suppose it's a long way off. I'll be retired by then.

I wonder how our four emissaries are faring? I trust they won't let anyone down…}

Chapter 10.

At morning break Phil, Sonja and I went to the canteen for a coffee.

The headmaster had given instructions that Sonja was not to be pestered even though, as the only girl in the school, she was an obvious source of interest. Phil the Bulldog took this seriously and positioned himself at the end of our table where he could make threatening faces at anyone who came too close yet still hear what we were saying. I told Sonja about the astronomer who was staying with us.

'I haven't seen him yet, he arrived early in the morning and was still asleep when I got up. Mum said his name was Matt.'

'Matt,' giggled Sonja. 'He's fun. He's young, probably the youngest there, most of them are much older.'

'You know him?' I asked.

'He's friendly, at least he is to me. He tried to talk to Karl once but he didn't get very far. I told him it wasn't his fault, Karl doesn't like to talk with people, he likes to talk at them.'

'What does this Matt look like?' asked Phil over his shoulder, not relaxing from his bulldog duties.

'Quite small, with blond hair like me,' said Sonja.

Phil and I thought exactly the same thing at exactly the same time. The man on the bus. It had to be him.

'He's not like the others,' continued Sonja. 'He works so hard he gets headaches and when he does he can't see properly. Apparently, the other night when he'd finished at his telescope he came straight out of the dome and forgot to turn. He fell straight into the pond!'

This was news. Apart from the very visible domes I had no idea of the layout of the observatory. The False Four who had gone up there would have seen all this already and much else and I felt even more annoyed than ever.

'Why is there a pond?' I asked.

Sonja thought about it. 'I don't know,' she finally decided, 'It's big though and there are goldfish swimming in it.'

I tried to understand why that was important. Perhaps the water cooled the atmosphere around the domes so visibility was improved. But if so why the fish?

'Professor Maclachlan told Matt to keep his eyes open in future until he had found his bed. I heard him say it.'

Matt must have taken his advice. Mum would surely have mentioned a dripping wet astronomer turning up at five o'clock in the morning. I told Sonja about our journey on the bus.

'You're a dogsbody when you're the youngest.' She sighed. 'I should know. He was probably ordered to run the errand to put the book in the library, maybe it was his punishment for falling in the pond.'

The observatory didn't sound too different from school. Professor Maclachlan was its headmaster and Matt was a naughty boy. I never imagined something like that would carry on once everybody grew up, but of course I only had Sonja's explanation so far. Once Matt woke and I met him I could ask for his version of events. The bell sounded for the next lesson. Sonja was going to be with us for the whole week.

She was better at maths than I was which came as a shock. She finished the page of questions we had been set and started talking to me. 'Why didn't you tell me you wanted to visit the observatory so much?'

This was something which could no longer be avoided. 'I'm fascinated by it.' My solving of the quadratic equations slowed alarmingly from its usual speed.

'Have you always been?'

'I've always been interested in astronomy and space and what's out there but I never thought an observatory would suddenly appear half a mile away from where I live.'

'Oh.' Sonja absorbed this. Then she said: 'You've made a mistake in the third line, here, look at my answer.' She pushed her book across and I pushed it straight back. 'Please yourself,' she said, mildly.

It was another two minutes before I got the answer and when I did she glanced across. 'Correct.' I started on the next problem.

'Matt will take you up with him.' I tried not to show any emotion.

'He's like that.' She sat back in her chair as if she had given me the secret of the universe. 'No, don't do it,' said Phil in anguish from his seat just behind.

'Ah,' said Mr. Harris, the maths teacher, 'I see someone is confident enough to have their work examined. Usual class rules apply, even though we have a stranger in our midst.' He studied Sonja's answers.

'Very good. No mistakes. Well, Gentlemen, this young lady from Sweden has raised the bar. I confidently expected one of you to come out on top but it seems the further north you go the better the Mathematical Mind.'

He intended this as a joke but no-one laughed. We knew what was coming next.

'Class Rules. In order to drive standards up we aspire to the level of the best. I set Exercise 25 to be completed now and if unfinished, you can take it home.'

I turned helplessly towards Sonja. It wasn't her fault. Things were probably different where she came from. It was my fault for not explaining our own class rule. If you could answer the questions *slow down.*

Phil never swore except in the direst emergency.

'Bugger,' he said.

{A strange place this English school, not like home at all. The teacher seems more like an adversary rather than someone who wants to help. And so sarcastic. But who am I to judge? I appear to have got everyone into trouble. Perhaps I should apologise?}

Chapter 11.

The novelty of Sonja had worn off by the end of the day and I think she knew it because at the school gates she said a quick goodbye then walked off hastily in the direction of the observatory.

Phil and I dawdled our way home. 'The Fatuous Four didn't come back,' he observed.

'I suppose we'll have to listen to them tomorrow,' I answered, 'Probably in assembly.' We walked on, sunk in gloom.

'I don't suppose Sonja could get us in,' Phil said eventually.

'No, that would just be asking for trouble.'

'What about your astronomer then? She could ask him for us or you could do it yourself.'

I had been thinking about this all day. The problem was I couldn't see how I was even going to meet him. His hours were all wrong. He was asleep when I got up and when I returned from school no doubt he would have already left for the observatory. He was only using the house as somewhere to sleep, all of his other requirements would be taken care of where he worked. Except perhaps breakfast, but he would eat that at one o'clock in the afternoon after his eight hours sleep. I thought about leaving him a note saying I was fascinated by astronomy and would like to talk to him about it but I didn't think he'd want to wait around for three hours just to please me. What would he do in my house for that amount of time for a start? He'd die of boredom.

'We won't meet each-other,' I told Phil, 'I've already worked it out.'

Phil stopped suddenly and turned to face me. 'What are you like at getting up in the morning?'

'Terrible,' I admitted. 'I always need more sleep. It's even worse now I'm not allowed my alarm clock because it makes too much noise. I only wake up when Mum pulls the curtains.'

'I can wake up when I want,' confided Phil, 'It's like I've got a clock inside my head. Before I go to sleep I tell myself what time I want to wake up and I do – to the minute.' He'd never mentioned this before.

'Are you sure? I mean it never fails?'

'Once in a blue moon. Probably because I'm growing.'

That seemed logical enough.

'In that case it's a shame he's not staying with you. You could wake up just before he came in, speak to him, and get an invite for us both.'

'The point is, he isn't,' said Phil urgently, 'But what if I came around to yours and woke you up. Then you could sneak out and meet him before he got to your house. And then you could say what you wanted to say.'

I studied Phil's face closely. He seemed perfectly serious. I continued to stare but his expression didn't change.

'How are you going to get out of your house at that time in the morning?'

'Easy, my bedroom's on the ground floor and my parents sleep even more heavily than you. You should hear my Dad's alarm clock, it sounds like Big Ben.'

Phil had almost talked me into it. Only one problem remained.

'How are you going to wake me up?'

Phil had been reading too many adventure books. 'I'll throw stones at your window!'

This was where the plan was going to fail. If he was going to wake me up his stones would have to smash the window. The consequences of that would be harsh.

'Won't work,' I told him. 'I'll think of some other way.' I turned to walk off.

But to his credit Phil had thought things through.

'Leave your window open. I'll use small stones.'

{He's my best friend but sometimes he needs a shove in the back if anything's to be done. It seems obvious to me how to meet his astronomer, David just doesn't get it sometimes, he makes things more difficult than they need be. It's better him popping the question, I'm happy to lay the groundwork. I'm Organisation Man. Dave will take it from there, he's better than me at thinking on his feet. There's only one thing that can go wrong I suppose. I hope he remembers to leave his window open.}

Chapter 12.

As expected there was no astronomer when I walked in. Mum had seen him though and had cooked him breakfast. He rose at one o'clock on the dot and was downstairs in the kitchen at half past one on the dot after a shower. I asked Mum what he said but all she could remember was talking to him about the village, the people in it, the pub, its opening hours and other trivia. Did he tell you about his discoveries I asked. No, I don't think so she said. I ate my tea and toast and fumed silently.

Dad was no help when he arrived home from work. Had Matt settled in? he asked Mum, was there anything else we could do for him? Yes he had, she replied and no he didn't mention anything but he did ask about the village and the pub and its opening hours… I groaned inside and ate my dinner.

Upstairs I did the extra maths homework provided for me courtesy of Sonja then put todays geography underneath yesterdays. Then I sat on the edge of my bed and looked out at the first stars to appear in the night sky. I knew them by name and as each appeared I said the name and wondered briefly what was happening on the planets I was certain orbited them. Finally, too many stars appeared all at once and I couldn't keep up. I bounced on the edge of the bed and experienced free-fall, the same as astronauts would feel when they flew into space and were in orbit. Of course, they would feel it all the time, my experience was cut short the moment I landed back on the bed. Dad was also experiencing something. He shouted up the stairs for me to stop.

I looked at my alarm clock. It was twenty past ten.

Meteorites were bombarding the Earth. They were causing immense damage to cities. London had been wiped out, Paris was gone, Uppsala took a direct hit but Sonja was on another holiday with Karl and she wasn't there. She would never go home now. Still they rained down. The world waited in fear for the Big One. The dinosaurs must have done the same, looking up at the sky in fear. Then the news came. It had been seen. The largest telescope on the planet had seen it and it was headed directly for the south of England. Astronomers fingers trembled in fear and they were almost unable to hold their pencils while they performed the calculation: no, it couldn't be true. The target was Herstmonceux. The asteroid was five miles wide and it was going to hit sooner than any warning could possibly be given. It was here now, its fireball was visible and it was moving fast. There would be no escape. Its sonic boom flattened everything ahead of the impact point and a microsecond later it fell on the unsuspecting village… I woke up with a start. It wasn't a dream at all, there were meteorites all around me on the bed. I sat up and another one came through the window narrowly missing my head. Then I remembered.

I scrambled to the window just in time to stop Phil launching another stone. 'Stop', I whispered as loudly as I could, waving my arms.

'About time,' he whispered back fiercely, caught in mid-throw. 'You could sleep through an earthquake. I've almost run out of stones. You'd better bring them down with you so we can repair your Mum's rockery!'

I didn't have to get dressed, I must have fallen asleep in my clothes. I gathered as many of the pebbles as I could carry and inched my way downstairs. The front door squeaked as I opened it. Phil didn't say anything when he saw me he just pointed to the damage. I placed the stones where I thought they should be and glared at him. Away from my house I started to breathe a little more easily.

'Quiet isn't it,' grinned Phil, 'Are you still sure you want to meet him?'

I hadn't been bombarded by half a rockery and woken up before dawn for nothing. 'Of course,' I said.

'Have you worked out what you're going to say to him?'

'No.'

'You've got about five minutes to think of something.'

We had passed the bus stop. The gate at the end of the drive leading to the observatory was ahead of us and it was open. We stopped. Phil looked at the gate. 'They probably leave it open because they don't trust him with a key, he might fall into the pond again and lose it.'

'Have you any idea,' I asked, suddenly desperate now the moment was upon me, 'What I should say? He'll be tired after a long night seeing new things and he won't be expecting this. How should I open the conversation?'

Phil thought for a moment then shrugged. 'I can't help you, I've done my bit. But whatever you manage to arrange make sure it includes me.' He added: 'I think its best I'm not around. I'll slip away when we're sure its him.'

I looked at Phil in alarm and was about to ask him why he wouldn't stay when we heard the crunch of gravel beneath someone's feet. The sound was getting louder. I dared to look around the corner and there he was, a small blond haired man walking towards me with his head down. He rubbed his eyes as he walked then looked up into the steadily lightening sky as if he hadn't seen enough of it yet and didn't want to miss anything. I gasped: 'It's him!'

But when I turned back Phil wasn't there.

I started to panic. What was the best way of doing this? I couldn't just jump out. Equally, it would look odd if I turned the corner just as he was about to come around it. What could I say? 'Hi, I'm out for a stroll, fancy meeting you here. By the way, my friend Phil and I were wondering if you would let us look through your telescope sometime in the near future.' All of a sudden this didn't seem like a good idea. His footsteps were getting closer. I shrank back into a bush that framed someone's drive and found out where Phil had vanished to by stepping on his toes.

'Ouch. This is my hiding place and there's no room for two!' Phil pushed hard sending me hurtling back out onto the pavement. He still hadn't appeared round the corner. I looked around wildly seeking somewhere else to hide…

And that's how he first saw me. Off balance and desperate. I saw the look of surprise on his face and I think he rubbed his eyes again. 'Hi,' I said, trying to muster some composure.

'Hello,' he replied, uncertainly.

There was no going back now.

{I nearly jumped out of my skin. Then I recognised him from a photograph in the house. He looked like he had been up to something he shouldn't but for the life of me I couldn't imagine what. I had been brought up in the city and this was the country. He was certainly up early though. Why did he look so nervous? Had I seen something I shouldn't, something I didn't even recognise? Now he was saying hello and he looked even more anxious. Well, if I don't talk to him I'll never find out why he appears so worried. I'll say hello back and see what happens.}

{Funny how the biggest things can have the smallest beginnings. You never realise what's happening when it is actually happening. Only years later when you look back do you know. Maybe that is a Law of the Universe. What would it be like if we did know? Not good, I suspect. People would be too afraid.}

Chapter 13.

We tried to keep it a secret from Sonja but she guessed something was up by our behaviour. For a start we couldn't stop smiling. But first we had to suffer more of her pyrotechnics in lessons.

Our pride had taken a small knock in geography and then a much larger one in maths but that was nothing compared to the hiding she dished out in physics. I suppose we should have expected it. Our only consolation was that our physics teacher, Dr. Symes, came off worse than us. In hindsight it was brave of him to choose that of all lessons to start talking about astronomy.

He began with the new radio telescope at Jodrell Bank. Sonja had been there, with Karl, and met its founder, Bernard Lovell.

Dr. Symes described our sun as an average star. Sonja agreed with his analysis as far as it went but then pointed out to the class recent ideas concerning the formation of elements heavier than hydrogen in the core of huge stars that blew up in gigantic explosions called supernovae. She had met the Burbages who had helped develop the theory only last year and they had explained it to her. We had no idea who these people were but Sonja's tales of fantastic detonations in outer space were extraordinary.

Dr. Symes made a final attempt. The Russians had launched Sputnik 1 and 2 a few months ago as we were all aware. He said the Russians were well ahead in the space race and would continue to be so.

Sonja smiled quietly and told him there was a difference between lobbing basketballs which beep into orbit and sending up satellites that do real science. The Americans had Explorer 1 on the launch pad and were waiting for final tests to be carried out before launching. It was carrying an experiment by someone called van Allen of whom we might hear more. Then she said President Eisenhower had ordered the creation of something called the National Aero… For the first time she stumbled over her words. She tried again. The National Aeronaut… She shook her head. The exact name wouldn't come to mind. Anyway, she did remember the initials. NASA. We might hear more of that in the future as well. To finish off Dr. Symes once and for all she mentioned she had met President Eisenhower.

Phil and I were agog.

'Why didn't you tell us all this before?'

Her answer was predictable.

'You never asked.'

'But how could we ask you something like that?' Phil the logician tried to impress upon her how unlikely it was.

'You didn't think this was my first holiday with Karl did you? As I said, he is an important man and he has made important discoveries. People want to hear about them.'

I remembered the look on Dr. Symes' face. He prided himself on his knowledge of recent developments and was forever trying to get us to subscribe to journals and magazines or if we couldn't afford that to at least obtain them from the library. His expression had been one of astonishment mixed with envy.

'He was so surprised he forgot to hand out homework,' I said.

Phil picked up on this quickly. 'We have history next, then art. Tell me you know more than the teachers and promise you'll say it all, it's getting near to the end of term, we don't need any more homework, we can't concentrate.'

Sonja laughed out loud. 'Of course I can't do that, if it's not astronomy then I'm learning as well. Anyway, why can't you concentrate? Are you excited because Santa is coming?'

Phil snorted.

‘Ok then,’ she said, ‘Now its your turn. Tell me what it is that has made you two so happy.’

We had to admire her. In a single bound she had deflected attention away from herself and back onto us. We just weren’t sophisticated enough to win a battle of wits with her. Maybe that ability also increased the further north you went. Phil and I looked at each other; she would find out soon enough anyway. I beckoned her close and dropped my voice to a whisper. ‘I spoke to Matt earlier today, in fact much earlier.’

Sonja didn’t react and I thought she hadn’t heard.

‘You know, Matt the astronomer. The one who’s staying at my house.’

‘Yes, I know who he is,’ she said. ‘What about him?’

Phil intervened. ‘Just before David takes all the glory you should know I thought of it. He can’t wake up in the morning.’ Phil’s idea of a whisper wasn’t mine. I signalled frantically that he should lower his voice to less than a million decibels.

‘Why are you waving your hands,’ Sonja asked. ‘Is it something to do with what you said to Matt?’ We were beginning to attract attention.

‘Tell her quickly,’ I groaned, ‘Before the whole school knows.’

Phil told her, quickly.

The final event of the day was a special assembly in the hall where the Fraudulent Four got to show off about their visit to the observatory. Sonja, Phil and I sat at the back on purpose where we could ignore them. Short of sticking our fingers in our ears however we couldn’t avoid all they said but I revelled in the negatives. They hadn’t looked through the telescopes, they hadn’t learned anything I didn’t know already and although they had been invited back to do some night-time observing a date hadn’t been set. We were going to beat them to it. The northside teachers checked regularly to see how I was taking it and I hope I annoyed them with my reaction. It wasn't a put on. I really couldn't have cared less.

{We wanted to annoy that idiot Smith and his friend Phil and their new friend Sonja and we looked while we were speaking but we didn't see them at first. Perhaps they were so overcome by envy they had sagged school and if so we hoped the teachers noticed they were missing and did something about it. Then they would be in even more trouble. We knew all about Smith's fascination with the observatory and how he was making a fool of himself. Teston would follow him anywhere, he was a miserable lump without an original idea inside his head. Why Sonja was with them we didn't know, it was just unlucky she met them first. She would have more fun with us if she only knew it. The pity was in a few days she was going. Given more time she would realise they were obsessed and we weren't, the good part for us was a day off school, the bonus was we could upset Smith at the same time. She didn't realise what a goody-two-shoes he had been before all this. The observatory was better than school but it wasn't all David Smith cracked it up to be. We put on an act just for him really, pretending it was amazing. Then we saw him, cowering at the back. Shame he hadn't bunked off. And then we looked closer. If we were putting on an act how much better was his? He didn't seem worried or envious, he was actually smiling. Pig. But it was only for show. Inside he must be in turmoil. We carried on with our presentation. We had been invited back (we finished with that). The headmaster looked very pleased and we reflected his beam back to the hall. Smith wouldn't look at us as we finished, we noticed that. But we also noticed something else. He hadn't stopped smiling}

Chapter 14.

That night it was easy because I didn't have to wake up.

Adrenaline kept me awake until I heard my parents go to bed at 11pm. Further adrenaline saw me through the next hour until it was time to leave for the rendezvous. A final burst of adrenaline hit me as I crept slowly down the stairs. How much of the stuff could your body produce? I felt more awake than I had ever been. Fortunately I wouldn't need any more. After this I would be seeing the Universe in close up and if that didn't stimulate me then nothing would.

Phil was around the corner. He dropped a handful of pebbles when he saw me. 'Just in case,' he said.

We walked to the gates of the observatory. Sonja was there.

'You have to put out your torches,' she said immediately. 'Why not leave them here? You can collect them on your way back.'

Extinguishing them left us in total darkness. Phil and I stumbled forward but Sonja had eyes like a cat because she guided us unhesitatingly up the drive towards the domes.

'You'll get used to it,' she giggled, 'Open your eyes as wide as you can and look upwards.'

We must have made a strange sight, Sonja confidently finding her way in the dark while Phil and myself fumbled, our necks craned, trying to look at the gaps between the stars, not the stars themselves, for fear their tiny pinpricks of light might dazzle us.

'It's very clear tonight,' said Sonja, 'There's hardly any mist. In an hour or so it will have vanished completely.'

I became conscious of the gravel crunching beneath my feet just as it had earlier when we had intercepted Matt. I had thought it loud then but now it was a hundred times louder, surely we couldn't fail to be heard? Sonja dismissed my worries.

'Light is the problem,' she assured us, 'Not sound. Some of them may have opened the domes by now to take initial calibrations and if you still had your torches with you they would know immediately and there would be big trouble.' In the dark she couldn't tell what impact her words had made but she wanted to make sure we understood so she emphasised it. 'Big Trouble… But sounds are nothing. Even Karl says it can be quite spooky observing for hour after hour in silence and he doesn't believe in anything supernatural. Still, he usually has some music to listen to and so do most of the others. In fact, so they can't hear anyone else's choice of music they often turn the volume up until it is quite loud. I can hear it drifting across when I'm trying to get to sleep.'

Our eyes were becoming accustomed to the darkness. Up ahead I could just distinguish the outline of a dome, not because it was giving out its own light but because it stood silhouetted against the rapidly vanishing remnant of the mist. I knew that directly beneath a telescope lay, pointed at the heavens. Sonja took us straight towards it.

It was dark inside as well but not completely so. As we crossed the threshold I saw someone hunched over looking down at a table with a tiny torch in his hand. His head was very close to the table and as we grew closer I could see what he was examining. It was a map but not an ordinary map. So engrossed was the figure in what he was doing he failed to notice us until we were standing right next to him.

'Hi Matt,' said Sonja.

The man straightened up. 'Hello.' He looked at Phil and I and smiled. 'I've had eight hours sleep since I last saw you two. Have you had any?'

The words I planned to say now stuck in my throat. I guess it was the same for Phil. We shook our heads.

'Then I'm impressed. You really are interested. Welcome to Herstmonceux.'

We stood there gazing at him. It was really happening. What I had dreamed about ever since I…

My train of thought was cut abruptly short. There were practicalities to be observed and absorbed. Matt shone his torch around and gave us a short guided tour.

'The entrance you just came through, I don't know if you noticed but there is a raised grille you stepped over, careful you don't trip over it.' He swung the beam to the left. 'Motors and electrics, don't touch anything there, the voltage is quite high.' Now it was half way around. 'Stairs to the observing level and a small but select library…' and finally back to the other side of the entrance, 'Storage cupboards, camera equipment, spare film and… Blankets!'

'Blankets,' repeated Phil.

'It gets cold in the early hours and I for one feel the cold. I set some sort of record last week for how many hours a day a person could be wrapped up in a blanket. I was in this dome for ten hours then wrapped up for an hour in the canteen because the heating had failed and then of course there's the eight hours I spend at your house sleeping. Makes a total of nineteen hours in a blanket. Can anyone beat that?'

He held the torch on the cupboard containing the blankets for a second longer but I knew he was only being dramatic. He, like me, was really only concerned with one thing inside the dome.

'Oh yes,' he mused, 'I almost forgot. There is something else of interest in here…'

He quickly swung the beam across and upwards and my eyes followed instinctively. He knew exactly where to point; I took a second to focus.

And there it was.

'Ohh.'

The sudden breath I took in was completely involuntary, a reflex I couldn't control. I had seen telescopes before but nothing like this. It was massive yet elegant, huge and impossibly suspended in mid-air defying gravity. I took a step back. Surely it must come crashing to the ground.

'It had that effect on me the first time I saw it,' said Sonja.

'It's so big,' I gasped.

Matt allowed the torch beam to run down the barrel all the way to the base of the telescope. It was grounded in a motor firmly anchored to the floor.

'The Yapp 36 inch reflector,' said Matt.

'Wow,' said Phil.

'Wow is right,' answered Matt proudly. 'This is the best telescope here, almost state of the art. It couldn't be used at Greenwich anymore because its mirror became tarnished with pollution but with a clean-up and a better site it's as good as new.'

'And you're allowed to use it?' I asked. I hadn't meant it to come out like that but Matt took it as a comment on his youthfulness.

'Yes,' he grinned, 'I am competent you know.'

I was still trying to take in the size of the instrument. 'Can we look through it?'

Matt nodded. 'You can, for about an hour before the mist clears completely and then I can use it myself. Step away from the wall.'

I wondered why we had to do that. Matt walked over to the telescope's control panel and I got my answer. With a sudden rumble of machinery the floor started to rise. Phil and I looked at him astounded.

'You weren't expecting that were you?'

Sonja chuckled. 'See, I didn't tell them,' she said to Matt, 'I remembered.'

The floor jerked to a halt. Matt operated more controls and now the telescope itself started to move. Slowly but not ponderously it settled into position and as it did so a crack in the dome overhead opened and grew wider. Through it we could see a slice of the night sky. The Yapp 36 inch reflector came to a halt pointing upwards at an angle of about 45 degrees directly below the gap in the dome. Matt put his eye briefly to a small barrel which protruded from the side and nodded to himself. He looked over at us.

'Come and see this!'

Phil and I ran. I got there first.

The hour passed in a flash. The first thing we saw was the moon but it was the moon as I had never seen it before. I could almost touch it. There were thousands of craters, not just Tycho and Copernicus which everybody knew but many, many others. Phil and I picked out one each and modestly named them after ourselves. I could have looked at that one image for hours.

But there was more. The telescope moved and Matt advised us not to look while it was doing so or we would get dizzy. When it stopped, there was Mars.

The planet really was red or at least orange. Matt checked and said we were lucky, surface features were visible, sometimes the whole planet was obscured by clouds of dust rising in huge storms. I had wanted to watch the moon for hours but now I wanted to watch Mars for hours instead. Matt gently pulled me away and the telescope swung again.

Jupiter and its Great Red Spot. The planet swam in front of me. On the surface I could see small round dots which were the shadows of its larger moons. It wasn't really the surface we were seeing Matt reminded us, it was the cloud tops. These clouds were made of chemicals different to Earth's atmosphere so we couldn't see through them. The thousand mile an hour winds had whipped them into coloured stripes and they were travelling so quickly that if you tried hard you could almost imagine you saw them moving. Matt tried to give us some idea of how far away Jupiter was. I didn't doubt his figures but I couldn't concentrate on what he was saying.

We were running out of time. Use of the telescopes was logged automatically and when observing conditions were right they must be used for research or the director of the group would want to know why not. The atmosphere was as clear as it was going to be and the heat from the ground had dissipated meaning that air was no longer convecting upwards.

'Just time for one more,' said Matt hurriedly looking at his watch, 'It would be a shame to miss this.'

We stood back while the telescope made its final move. Matt had no time to check its positioning, instead, as soon as it stopped, he waved me towards the eyepiece. 'Don't take too long,' he said, then added, 'But do enjoy it.'

I looked.

And there was Saturn.

I had never seen anything so beautiful in my life.

{I've been a working astronomer for thirty-five years, directing my group for fifteen, and with that much experience you get a feel for what should be happening with the telescopes in your charge. So when the Yapp started to move when it shouldn't I knew something out of the ordinary was happening. I had a good idea who was in that dome but I checked the duty list just to be sure – it was who I had thought. I tapped out my pipe and took a stroll out of the administration building. The door to the dome was open, unusual in itself if serious observation was occurring, and as I walked closer I heard excited voices. I stopped. Now I had two choices.

I knew what I should have done. There were strict rules regarding when the public could visit and even stricter rules about who was allowed to be present when the telescopes were in use and I should know: I wrote them. So the first choice was to interrupt what was going on, remove the trespassers and discipline Matthew Day. That was my responsibility, in fact it was more than that, it was my obligation. I didn't move.

Instead I remembered how it had been for me when I was young. I tried to recapture the same excitement and it was there but too much time had got between us and it was faint, an echo across the years. I looked up at the Universe.

The Yapp pointed straight at the full moon. What sights they must be seeing. Matthew was taking them on the Grand Tour of the Solar-System and he still had an hour to go. I turned away.

The second choice was the correct one. I would have a quiet word with Matt Day about all this. But not tonight.}

Chapter 15.

Just after half-past one in the morning the real work began.

Matt directed the telescope to look at the Andromeda galaxy, something he said he always did to calibrate his nights work. He allowed us a brief look but after that he had a programme of observations which he said he must complete before the sky grew too light again. That gave him just under five hours and while what he did seemed exciting to him to the rest of us it wasn't. When he had time he apologised and tried to explain what he was doing.

'I'm looking at Active Galaxies. They don't look like much at visible wavelengths but they also emit at wavelengths we can't see. The ones I'm interested in aren't quiet like our galaxy, they have events occurring in them which are enormously powerful and I'm trying to understand what is going on.'

We nodded politely.

'We're lucky to be where we are in the Universe. You wouldn't want to live in those places.'

Astronomy for Matt didn't consist of looking in wonder through the telescope though he seemed to gain just as much satisfaction as we had earlier. He didn't say so directly but it was obvious we didn't know enough to fully appreciate his work. Even Sonja yawned after an hour.

'You should go to bed,' Matt chided.

'So should they,' she said instantly.

I shook my head. 'I can't. I'd wake everyone up and get into big trouble.' My only hope was to sneak in with Matt when he returned to my house. Phil shrugged.

'I can go home if you like; unless I set a bomb off no-one will know I've been out.'

That made Matt laugh. He thought for a moment. 'I've an idea. There are plenty of blankets in the cupboard and it's a mild night so I'm not going to need any. If you want to get a few hours' sleep I can continue with what I'm supposed to be doing then when it becomes too light for me to carry on I'll wake you up.'

That solved my problem so I nodded agreement. Phil and Sonja looked at the floor the blankets would be on and I could see them comparing it to their soft comfortable beds. They didn't look happy. Matt had turned away and so couldn't see this but I needn't have worried. In the throwaway style I was becoming accustomed to he suddenly made three hours on a wooden floor seem like the most desirable thing in the world.

'One thing you should know. When it's too light for me to see distant galaxies it's still dark enough so this telescope can detect comets before they become obvious. We'll have about half an hour for you to do that if you wish.'

We perked up immediately. Then he played his trump card.

'And don't forget – If you find a comet you get to name it…'

I didn't think I would sleep but I was wrong. I dreamt of discovering a comet and becoming famous. My fame took me way beyond having a special school assembly, I was on television, on the new astronomy programme The Sky at Night. As it was a dream I wasn't at all nervous and ended up being asked to present it instead of the astronomer who's idea it had been, someone called Patrick Moore, who agreed readily. I was so good the programme didn't stop at the normal time but carried on into the small hours of the morning while I talked knowledgeably about active galaxies for ages. My headmaster, who was watching, rang up to say it was obvious I was wasting my time at school and I could leave immediately.

'Why are you smiling?'

I struggled to fit this unexpected remark into the show. The TV camera pointed straight at me waiting for an answer.

'Wake up!'

Phil was leaning over me and was shaking me by the shoulder. I opened my eyes and the dream evaporated. I stopped smiling.

'I'm sorry I had to wake you up, you looked so content.'

The best dreams sometimes happen under the strangest circumstances. I looked at Phil. It would have been pointless trying to explain. Phil impressed the urgency of the situation on me. 'Are you going to get up? Matt says we can comet hunt now!'

We didn't find a comet but we laughed while Matt made the telescope swing to and fro and told us how he doubted it had had as much fun since it was made.

'This really is a shot in the dark,' he said then smiled as he realised what he'd said. 'Anyway, if you ignore the bad pun, it's very unlikely we'll catch a comet doing this, we'd have to be fantastically lucky, we'd actually have to find one with a tail and if it was that close to the sun it would have been spotted already. There are thousands of amateur astronomers and they wouldn't all miss it.'

'So we're wasting our time,' complained Phil.

'Not quite.' Matt tried not to sound hurt by the remark. 'I hope you get the point that comets can appear from anywhere, there's no preferred direction. That's why we looked in so many different places.'

'But what if you really wanted to find one,' persisted Phil, 'What would you do then?'

'Use a method that goes back years,' answered Matt, 'The same method Clyde Tombaugh used to discover Pluto. The Blink Comparator.'

'What's that?' said Phil, 'I've never heard of it.'

Matt looked at his watch but it could only have been reflex which made him do so. Observation was ending for the night and around us the domes were closing. It was half past six in the morning. 'It will have to wait until next time,' he said, 'But we do have one here and we can use it.'

'When?' I asked.

Matt sounded surprised. 'Tomorrow night of course. I thought you were coming along every night until Sonja leaves. That's what she told me.'

Sonja had been unusually quiet while our conversation had been going on and now we realised why. She must have been expecting it to end with this question. I looked at Phil and to his credit he rose to the occasion.

'Yes, that's right. I hope that's ok with you Matt.'

I quickly joined in. 'It's very kind of you.'

Matt paused, probably thinking for the first time that he had only Sonja's word we were allowed to keep such late hours. He said: 'It's all agreed with your parents of course…?'

We assured him it was. Sonja breathed a small sigh of relief and changed the subject.

'You haven't told us how you know comets come from any direction,' she said to Matt.

'Oh. Well, briefly, it's because of a theory by Oort which says that comets exist in a cloud, the Oort cloud, around one light year outside the solar system. The cloud is perturbed from time to time making comets fall toward the sun and when they do they heat up and evaporate leaving some of their matter spread out for millions of miles behind them. It's this matter that we see as the comets tail. According to Oort his cloud is spherical so we can expect comets to enter the solar system from random directions. It's a good theory. It matches observation.'

Phil and I paused to digest this.

Sonja didn't. She had been itching to speak all the time Matt had been explaining. Now she had her chance. 'Are you talking about Jan Hendrik Oort?'

Matt nodded, 'That's right.'

'Thought so,' said Sonja as she looked out of the entrance to the dome.

'Don't tell us,' I said, 'You've met him.'

But she had gone. In the distance I swore I heard her give another of her infuriating giggles.

{A Comet! A Comet!! A Comet!!!

We're going to find a comet. Correction, I'm going to find a comet and I'm going to name it!

I'm going to be more famous than Karl. And because I'm younger I'll have more time to discover more than him. I'll have a head start. He'll never catch me up.

It's really going to happen.

A Comet!!!!}

Chapter 16.

Phil and I walked home with Matt. Although he hadn't spent much of his time actually looking through the telescope the evening's observing had obviously taken its toll because he stopped several times to rub his eyes just like he had the first time I had seen him leave the observatory. He apologised each time and muttered something about how it was getting worse and that he should get an eye-bath to use before he went to sleep. His eyes felt dry he explained, perhaps it was the local atmospheric conditions.

Phil said goodnight then said good morning when he remembered what time it was. Matt advised him on sleeping patterns before he left. 'If you're really going to come along try to fit sleep around whatever else you have to do during the day. I understand school hasn't broken up yet?'

Phil pulled a face.

'If I were you I'd go straight to bed now and get a good couple of hours. You'll feel tired during the day but you'll just have to get through that. Have an early evening meal then sleep again, that should be enough before you get up at midnight. Remember two things: It's the total number of hours that you get which is important, it doesn't matter when they are during the day.'

'I'll sleep in lessons,' Phil told him, 'No-one will notice, I tend to keep my head down anyway.'

I wondered what the second thing to remember was so I asked. Matt put on his serious face but he did this when he wasn't being serious as well as when he was so it was difficult to tell how much importance to attach to what he said. It was a quirk of his I had noticed.

'The second thing you can't do to order but it's a big help if you can', he answered mysteriously. We waited but he didn't go further.

'What?' said Phil impatiently, 'What is it?'

Matt smiled. 'Simple,' he said, 'Try to dream. It tidies up your mind.'

Matt had a key to my house and we entered. All was silent. I stepped inside behind him but it would have been better if I'd gone to sleep in the garden shed instead. Shandy was usually the worst guard dog in the world, the previous night she hadn't stirred when Matt had arrived and normally she would ignore me too. But this wasn't normal and she was curious. She asked me where I had been and what I'd done and could she perhaps come along next time to share in the fun. The trouble was she said it in her language and she didn't know how to whisper. By the time I'd quietened her there was movement at the top of the stairs.

'David? Is that you?'

'Good dog,' I hissed, waving my fist at her.

She put a paw on my hand and stared at me solemnly.

'It is you,' said Mum's voice sounding surprised. 'I suppose you know what time it is; you have two hours to plan your excuse, please make it a good one.' Her bedroom door closed. Matt and Shandy stared at me.

'Two hours,' I moaned, 'I'll need two decades to talk my way out of this.'

'I thought you had permission?' said Matt. When I didn't answer he gave me his final piece of advice for the night.

'You've got no choice, you'll have to tell the truth.'

Two hours later I took his advice.

{What's the point of shouting at him? When he was a baby he kept me awake for longer so in a way this is an improvement. Shouting will only turn him against me and he'll do it again anyway. I've never seen him so excited. I'll be practical. I'd like to look through those telescopes myself but I don't suppose I'll be welcome, he's at that age where he won't acknowledge me directly in public but still depends on me for so many things… I've heard it called 'difficult' but it's not really. 'Obvious' would be a better name. What do people expect? Apron strings and all that. Practical then. He has to go to school as well and I can't afford another letter home, the next one might be an invitation for me to see the headmaster and apron strings or no apron strings there are limits.

But one thing is certain. Now that the house is quiet again I'm not staying awake for two hours thinking about it. I'm going back to sleep. The correct thing to do will occur to me before I wake up. If I'm honest with myself I already know it. (No darling, it's only Matt. Go back to sleep.)}

Chapter 17.

At five minutes to midnight that night I decided it would have been better if I hadn't. I had been embarrassed for one hour and twenty minutes and I still was.

Once again Mum had been reasonable about everything. What was it with parents? If you give them time to think they became sensible. When they don't have time they react like you think they will and shout and threaten. I wondered how long it had taken Mum to see things from my point of view. Certainly not the two hours I had stayed awake planning what I was going to say. When I came down to breakfast she said she had gone back to sleep almost immediately.

'It looks like you're not going to stay away from the observatory no matter what I say,' she began. 'So I've worked out how you can do it and still get enough sleep to function properly in school.'

I counted how many hours I'd already been awake. It would have been two less if she'd said this when I first disturbed everyone.

'When you get home you'll go straight to bed. Then I'll wake you up for tea and after you've eaten you can do your homework. You won't be able to lie down straight away, you won't digest your food properly.'

I nodded.

'Then you can go to bed again. You'll be able to have another four hours before you leave here at twelve, then when you get back you can have another two hours before breakfast. Shandy won't make such a noise again, I'll have a word.'

It was uncanny. She must have read Matt's mind.

I spooned cornflakes into my mouth in an attempt to escape but it was difficult to eat them quickly as the milk was scalding hot.

'Now.' She became businesslike.

The roof of my mouth hurt and a small sliver of skin just behind my front teeth burnt off and dangled where my tongue could feel it.

'Food.'

It was like being at a particularly well-organised Scout camp.

'If you have to be awake most of the night you'll need something to keep you going. Your body isn't used to it normally so we'd better make arrangements. Before I go to bed at ten-thirty I'll make you a flask of tomato soup and wrap some corned beef sandwiches, no matter when you eat them the soup will still be hot but make sure you don't forget. Do you think I should provide some for the others?'

I didn't answer.

'Maybe not, no sense in making them dependent on me.'

I spooned the hot milk into my mouth as fast as could. It burned all the way down but I didn't care.

'They'll get the idea. Then they can make their own arrangements.'

Dad came downstairs. 'Morning,' he said to me then glanced at the front door and tried to make a joke.

'No more letters from Dowding I see, looks like you're doing something right. Keep it up.'

Now it was exactly midnight and time to go. I glared at the flask of soup and the neatly packed rounds of sandwiches. I didn't dare leave them.

'How did Tombaugh discover Pluto?' Matt repeated my question. We were in what I called the 'Golden Hour' when we could have some fun with the telescope before Matt had to get down to his serious work. 'It's quite straightforward. He used one of these.'

Matt was standing by a device we hadn't noticed before. It was a small table upon which were two large astronomical photographs and above which was what looked like a double-barrelled microscope. He beckoned me over.

'How wide apart are your eyes?' he asked. I had no idea.

'Never mind, we'll do it by trial and error.'

He made me look down both barrels, one eye to each and adjusted the gap. 'Is that comfortable?'

I was looking straight down at the photographs but each eye was receiving the image of only one. I knew that was the case because he told me so but down the microscope it was as if both eyes were looking at exactly the same image. The photographs were negatives, the stars were black dots and the space between them white.

'What do you see?'

'No difference.'

'Ok, try this.' Matt switched the machine on and it made a clicking sound. 'Now look again.'

I looked. There was still no difference, though now it was apparent that each eye was being shown one of the photographs alternately and the machine was switching between them rapidly.

'Look carefully.'

Then I saw it. All of the black dots remained in their positions as the comparator ticked except one. This dot jumped from one place to another then back again at exactly the same rate as the ticking. It was the only dot to do so. It's displacement wasn't great but it was easily noticeable once you saw it for the first time.

'Congratulations,' said Matt, 'You've just discovered Pluto!'

'Let me look,' asked Phil and took my place. He saw it immediately. 'Wow!'

'These are copies of the plates Clyde Tombaugh used,' said Matt. 'They're a piece of astronomical history. Pluto was the last planet in the solar system to be discovered and it wasn't all that long ago. 1930.'

'Do you think others will be discovered,' asked Phil, not taking his eyes from the flickering image.

'It's possible,' admitted Matt, 'But unlikely. Any such planet has escaped detection even though versions of this machine are readily available to professionals and amateurs throughout the world. If there is another it must either be very small or have an orbit which is extremely unusual as its managed to hide itself for twenty-seven years. There probably isn't another planet out there despite what people would like to believe. We're better off searching for comets.'

Matt replaced the photographs with two others. 'These were taken two nights apart last week. If a comet is there and it's reasonably close it should be possible to see it.'

For the first time Sonja took an interest. She quickly jumped down from where she had been watching and hurried over. 'My turn,' she informed us, 'Excuse me.' Phil had been ready to launch the comet search himself and started to protest but Sonja was having none of it.

'You've just learned how to use the comparator,' she said, 'So now we're all equal because Matt and I already know.' She looked at Matt seeking confirmation but Matt had turned his back to us and seemed more interested in observing stars through the gap in the dome without the aid of a telescope.

'Yes, well it's true. And we must have equal time otherwise it's not fair.' She paused. 'It's not my fault that you had to learn.'

Phil moved away from the comparator and said something which I couldn't hear clearly though it might have been 'Glory Hunter'. Sonja ignored him and took his place at the instrument.

I watched her with a mixture of amazement and envy. Why was she behaving like this?

Matt had found something demanding his attention as far away from Sonja as possible. As she was monopolising the comparator Phil and I went over to see what it was. It wasn't anything, he just wanted to tell us something out of Sonja's hearing.

'Don't be too hard on her, it not her fault. She has a lot to live up to.' Phil made a sound half way between contempt and scorn but I understood.

'It's Karl isn't it?' I said, 'She's trying to compete with him.'

Matt nodded. 'One day she will learn she doesn't have to but right now...'

I looked over to where Sonja was working the comparator. It wouldn't have mattered if Matt hadn't taken his precaution, she was so fully absorbed she wouldn't have heard. She worked the machine furiously. I felt sympathy for her, it couldn't be easy being the daughter of a world-famous astronomer. I understood her name dropping just as I understood her frantic movements trying to discover something which Karl hadn't. In a few minutes when she was through she would lean away from the machine then walk back to the entrance to the dome where she would stand looking out into the darkness and brooding. The comparator had given her a chance and it still may allow her victory but not this time.

Phil scrambled towards the comparator and eagerly looked into it. Sonja may have missed something and if she had he was going to find it. I let him try. I had seen the fury with which she had worked.

When he finished he asked me if I would like to take over but I declined.

I knew there would be nothing to find.

{She certainly is Karl's daughter, you can see that in the same way she is driven: just like him. I wonder what he's really doing here? To give a talk, that's what he says but I wonder if there's more to his visit than that. So far as I know he hasn't asked to use our telescopes yet but that could change. And if he does what will Maclachlan say? Will he dare to refuse the redoubtable Professor or will he be as overawed as we're all supposed to be?

It's funny watching the boys with her, I don't think they realise what she has to live up to. She must have inherited his competitiveness. No-one could blame her if she settled for reflected fame.

I wonder what he's working on right now? He certainly isn't giving much away, the title of his talk is 'Recent Developments in Astronomy' which is pretty much a red rag to a bull and I'm sure he knows it. He's keeping his cards pretty close to his chest. I wonder if Sonja knows anything and if she does would she tell me? Do I dare ask?

No. Who wants to win like that. I can just see Karl's face if I scooped him with a trick. He's not one to forgive and his reputation for a quick temper goes before him. I wonder who'd come off worse, me or Sonja?}

Chapter 18.

The next day was cloudy. The weather forecast had warned it might continue through the night but that had been at six o'clock in the evening just before I went to bed. There was a vague promise it might clear later but I was sitting at my bedroom window at ten to midnight and I could see no stars. If the clouds were going to clear they hadn't yet.

I sat glumly, waiting. The clouds were thick and they didn't even look like they were going to blow away. I opened my bedroom window but the air wasn't moving. It was still chilly though, so after a while I pulled the window shut and sat breathing on the cold glass watching my breath condense until there was so much it formed drops of water which ran down the pane streaking through the film I had formed. I was so occupied with this I forgot what the time was.

There was sudden movement outside. I was startled but it was only Phil waving his arms. I quickly looked at my watch. Twelve fifteen. I hurriedly rubbed at the window until I was sure Phil could see me mime a reply then I hastily pulled on my coat.

I reached the front door and was just about to open it when I saw a note had been stuck on the inside. 'Don't Forget Your Provisions.' I turned back into the kitchen and there they were on the table.

'Why are you late?' asked Phil, 'Were you asleep?' He didn't sound annoyed, he just sounded as if he had got one up on me.

'No I wasn't,' I protested.

'Can't handle the pace?' he continued as if he hadn't heard me.

'I told you, I was awake.' I said this more firmly for his benefit and before he could say anything else I carried on: 'I was just wondering whether or not to bother tonight, it's been cloudy all day and it looks like it's not going to clear. I thought you might think that as well and not come along.'

'It takes more than a bit of cloud to stop a Real Astronomer,' Phil said, but for once he was wrong.

When we arrived the tops of the domes were shut. Matt was there with Sonja and they were looking at pictures he had taken the previous night. Matt had a large magnifying glass which he was moving over the photographs and he was dictating to Sonja, who was taking notes.

'Nothing doing tonight,' he greeted us as we entered. 'Too cloudy. One of the few nights this happens down here.'

'See,' I whispered to Phil, 'Clouds do stop Real Astronomers.'

Matt put down the magnifying glass and Sonja looked grateful. 'What's in your bag?' Matt asked, eyeing it curiously.

'Enough tomato soup and corned beef sandwiches to sink a battleship,' I said and he laughed.

'So there's more than a thimbleful each unlike last night,' he said. 'Things are looking up.'

I don't know if he meant that to be funny because looking up seemed like the last thing we were going to do. Matt pushed his pictures aside to make room on the desk. 'Let's make a start then, just the thought of it is making me hungry!'

As we ate Matt told us about the other astronomers and their areas of interest. Eventually he got round to Professor Maclachlan and at the mention of his name I perked up.

'He spoke to my Father in the pub and got him to agree that you could stay with us,' I said.

'I know,' said Matt munching on a sandwich, 'I'm very grateful.'

Sonja was unimpressed. ‘He’s an old fossil,’ she told us, ‘He doesn’t like me much, he can hardly bring himself to say good morning never mind pass the time of day.’

‘He has a lot on his mind,’ chided Matt, ‘So he doesn’t mean to be rude. He probably finds it difficult to know what to say to you.’

‘Why?’

‘Well,’ Matt waved his sandwich at her, ‘You’ve almost certainly met more important people than he has so he’s probably in awe of you.’

For a moment I thought Sonja believed him and she might have if he’d kept his face straight but a smile burst out.

‘Ha,’ said Sonja.

‘Give him a chance,’ urged Matt, ‘He’s not so bad. Listen, I’ll tell you what he’s working on right now, it might make you change your view.’ Matt paused and took a sip of tomato soup. Sonja made a point of turning away. Matt swallowed his soup but still didn’t speak and Phil couldn’t wait any longer.

‘Well?’

Matt put down his cup. ‘I’ll tell you. Little Green Men.’ That was enough to make Sonja turn back around.

‘Pardon?’ she said.

‘Flying Saucers!’

‘OOH!’ Phil let out such an exclamation that it startled us all. ‘I knew they were real,’ he said breathlessly, ‘I knew it.’

We stared at him wide-eyed while he tried to regain his composure. There were so many things he wanted to say about this and by the look of him he was going to say them all at once. To make sure none of us broke in with something of our own he repeated the noise he had made while his brain sorted it all out.

‘OOH!’

'I *knew* they were real, I saw Earth Versus the Flying Saucers last year at the cinema and I knew they were trying to tell us something...'

'The Saucers were?' I asked innocently.

'No,' Phil said, not rising to the bait, 'They were fake but only because the real ones don't want to be filmed, the director was telling us that they're visiting our planet and if he's right they're probably not friendly.'

I hadn't seen the film though I knew Phil had, but when he told me about it he hadn't been like this. It must have been playing on his mind.

'They wanted to take over the Earth. They didn't though because we figured out a way to stop them. But that was in the film, we might not be so lucky in real life.' Phil turned to Matt. 'Is that what Professor Maclachlan is working on? A way to stop them?'

'I don't think so,' answered Matt, 'He hasn't detected any yet.'

Phil was not impressed. 'That's what he told you.'

Sonja, for once, couldn't quote a higher authority so she was on her own. 'I don't believe anyone visiting us would be unfriendly like that. You don't realise how far away other planets are, flying saucers would have to travel millions of miles and when they got here they wouldn't want to start a fight, they'd be much more likely to want to be friends and share their knowledge.'

Matt tried to speak. 'Well…'

But Sonja had more to say. 'It would be more like Forbidden Planet. They'd have robots like Robbie and they'd try to save us from things we shouldn't know about. People would try to find out their secrets but they'd protect their knowledge and so protect us.'

Phil had been looking at Sonja. 'That's not what happened in Forbidden Planet. The seeds of destruction of the Krell were passed on and the humans were lucky to survive.'

Sonja stared back at him witheringly. 'It's a movie, they had to make it dramatic. Can't you use some imagination?'

Matt cleared his throat but before he could begin I felt it was my turn.

'You're both wrong, they wouldn't try to help us, if they'd come that far they'd want something from us and by the way they hide themselves it must be something we wouldn't want to give.' That dealt with Sonja. 'And, Phil, they wouldn't start a fight out in the open because it takes too much effort to even send their saucers so how could they afford to have even one blown up?' I looked around in triumph. 'No,' I said shaking my head, 'It would be like Invasion of the Body Snatchers. The saucer would drop pods down which would grow into things that looked just like us but they'd really be plants just like the saucer pilots themselves. They'd do away with real people and then, when there were enough of them, they'd take over everywhere. Imagine that! A whole planet conquered without a shot being fired.'

'Imagine a plant flying a saucer,' said Sonja unkindly. 'You should listen to yourself.'

'It's not a plant like on Earth,' I said hotly, 'It's a special type of plant, one with intelligence.' I thought for a second. 'Anyway there are plants here which can move so they might be intelligent. Think of the Venus Fly-Trap.'

'Have you ever seen one?' Sonja demanded.

I hadn't but I wasn't going to say so. I set my mouth in a firm line.

'If you were an inch long it could catch you,' she said scornfully, 'And they can't grow any bigger because then they wouldn't work.'

'Which shows what you know,' I said. 'You're limiting yourself to what's evolved on Earth. *You* should use some imagination and think what could have evolved on other planets with less gravity.'

By the look in Sonja's eyes she was preparing a speech about why I was hopelessly wrong. A long speech. Matt took the opportunity to jump in and say what he had been waiting to say.

'All those ideas have something going for them,' he began, diplomatically, 'But Professor Maclachlan is still in the early stages of planning to look for evidence of extra-terrestrial intelligent life. He hasn't found any flying saucers and he certainly isn't trying to cover up anything.' Matt rubbed his eyes. He blinked at us. 'He is in contact with Frank Drake. Have you heard of him?'

Sonja looked blank.

'Frank Drake is an astronomer who looks at the sky using radio telescopes. Just as I can see millions of stars through the Yapp he can see millions of radio sources using his equipment and because stars give out radio waves as well as light he's often looking at the same things.'

'Intelligent stars?' said Phil. 'Broadcasting radio?'

Matt rubbed his eyes again and smiled.

'You're almost there. A lot can be found out about stars by looking at every type of wave they emit including radio. Drake's idea, supported by Professor Maclachlan, is that the planets orbiting those stars will also be radiating radio waves if they contain intelligent life and he thinks he can pick up those transmissions. After all, the direction to point the radio telescope is already obvious. We can see the stars and the planets will be very close to them.'

I was astounded. We couldn't be that close to actually detecting life in the Universe. This was better than any of the films we had seen. 'When will they start?' I asked.

‘Soon,’ said Matt. ‘Drake has accepted a post at the National Radio Astronomy Observatory in West Virginia and he’s come up with an Equation and a Project. He’s told Maclachlan about both and the Professor told me.’

It even beat chasing comets. ‘Tell us,’ I demanded, ‘Tell us about all of it!’

‘I will,’ said Matt, ‘I just need a breath of fresh air.’

It wasn’t hot in the dome but I suppose the tomato soup could have warmed Matt up so much that he needed to cool off. Perhaps we should have drank it later on when it wasn’t so scalding.

Matt made his way to the entrance to the dome and stood for a moment, breathing. Then he stepped outside. Moments later there was a loud splash.

{I knew what had happened as soon as I heard the noise. I knew who it was as well. The first time had been amusing but now… Other people were running toward the sound. Oh no, I groaned as I saw who else was there, Matt had done it in front of those kids he’d invited. I really should have told him not to allow them up here again but the time had never seemed right. I blamed myself; some leader I had turned out to be.

Well it stopped now. It would have to anyway and not just because of this. No-one had mentioned anything to me so far but I had eyes in my head and I had noticed. Something was bothering Matt and he must be aware of it even though he said nothing. His colleagues had to have suspected something was not right but they were a loyal bunch and if Matt kept quiet they would too.

I would have to take some decisions. These kids, looking so worried as I approached them, would have to be disappointed. They would understand, in time. What to do about Matt himself was something else. I’ll have to take him off observation duties for a start. Then we would see when he could return. I was close enough to call out to them now, they mustn't just run away. How to break it to Matt?}

Chapter 19.

School the following day should have been a happy occasion because it was the last day of term but we couldn't be happy because we didn't know what had happened to Matt.

What must have been everyone at the observatory had rushed to find out what had occurred. The fact that no-one was doing any actual observing helped but even had they been Matt's shouts would just as surely have brought them running. The water wasn't deep and he easily dragged himself to the side once he realised where he was but by then the damage was done. We arrived at the same time as Professor Maclachlan who, once he had made sure Matt wasn't injured, took a dim view of us.

The Professor had sent us on our way. He said he hadn't been aware we had been observing and he said he would have strong words with Matt about it but now wasn't the right time.

'Did you wake anyone up when you got home,' Phil asked me.

'No,' I told Phil. 'But I didn't get much sleep. How about you?'

'I didn't sleep at all. I wonder what's wrong with Matt?' For the answer we had to wait for Sonja to appear.

We thought she wasn't coming at all until she arrived at break. She had something to tell us but she didn't want to be overheard so instead of coffee in the canteen we went for a walk in the bright winter sunshine. 'You know that's the second time Matt's fell in the pond don't you?'

'Yes,' said Phil, 'You told us.'

'Well, the first time it was a joke. Everyone including Matt thought it happened because the place was new and he just lost his bearings but Karl told me the Professor has now asked Matt what happened and Matt said he couldn't remember.'

‘Perhaps he banged his head,’ I said. ‘That can make you lose your memory.’

‘Apparently there was no bruise. Anyway, Professor Maclachlan told Matt he should see a doctor in the morning so that’s where he’s gone.’ That concluded all the news Sonja had.

‘What did Maclachlan say about you… and about us?’ I asked.

‘Karl wouldn’t say. I think that’s because it’s not good news but he probably thought I was already upset and didn’t want to make me even more unhappy.’

‘Then that looks like the end of our observing,’ said Phil gloomily. ‘They’ll probably find some way of blaming it on us anyhow.’ Phil turned to me. ‘Maybe it was your soup, maybe drinking too much of it makes you black out.’

‘Don’t be an idiot,’ I told Phil.

Sonja looked serious. ‘Phil’s right. Karl says those were the exact words the Professor used when he questioned Matt. ‘Did you black out?’ he wanted to know.

‘What did Matt say?’

‘He said he wasn’t sure.’

The only good thing to come out of it all was the failure of the Fatuous Four to go on their follow-up visit to the observatory. Matt was to have been their host but obviously that wouldn’t happen now. They didn’t take it well, especially as rumours of our visits were beginning to circulate. They found us at the end of break and tried to make something of it but Phil just stared at them and in the end they slunk off.

Meanwhile the teachers were trying to give us some fun. End of term quizzes were popular with the staff and Mr. Lewis had announced one for our final geography lesson. Mr. Lewis had also decided to handicap Sonja out of the quiz and we should have guessed something was wrong when he perched his spectacles on the end of his bony nose and, having announced Question One, opened his copy of Wisden. Question One concerned C.B. Fry's batting average. The rest of the questions were also about cricket. Sonja didn't score a single point and throughout seemed amused, if baffled.

Mr. Lewis hadn't quite finished. After the class had left with his false 'Happy Christmas' ringing in their ears he kept me back and reminded me about the homework I had failed to hand in. Another letter was on the way home. If homework failed to appear on the first day of next term I would be sorry.

'What did he want?' asked Phil, who had waited for me.

'Nothing important,' I replied.

The day ended earlier than usual. Phil and I walked Sonja back to the entrance to Herstmonceux but we didn't dare go any further. It had started to snow and large white flakes fell softly and vertically from the sky, drifting down and settling on us where they melted and on the ground where they remained. Sonja chose the moment to drop the first of three bombshells.

'I have to go away for a while. Karl is visiting Jodrell Bank, there's a new telescope there not like the ones here. He says it's very important and he has to see it.' The snow came down more heavily. We said goodbye and told her to contact us as soon as she returned.

When I arrived home the second bombshell hit. 'I've had a phone call from the observatory,' Mum said matter of factly. 'A Professor. I forget his name. He says Matt won't be staying here anymore, they've found room for him up there so that's probably a good thing. We won't have to creep around anymore in the morning.' I went upstairs to my room. As I sat looking out of the window the third bombshell suddenly hit me.

I wasn’t going to Herstmonceux that night or ever again. Through something which was nobody’s fault the most exciting time of my life was over.

I usually loved it when it snowed.

This time I cried.

{Something’s happened up there but David won’t tell me about it. I know he’s upset but I can’t do anything to help, he’ll tell me in his own time or not at all. It has to do with Matt, that much is obvious, but what can it be? I can’t ask David directly he’ll just clam up. Why did they have to come here anyway and disturb everything? I wish they’d never built the place.}

Chapter 20.

Matt told me to dream so I did.

I dreamt everything was like it was. Phil was there and Sonja too and so was Matt, everything was just like it was… but better. We were excited by something Matt had found and he left it to me to make the final confirmation. 'I can't be sure,' he said, 'You must take a look.'

There it was. I could be sure because I could do anything. On a piece of paper I sketched what I could see and added coordinates so there would be no mistake. My hand worked quickly and accurately even though I wasn't looking at it, my attention was fully on what I could see peering down the stereo microscope. Matt came and looked over my shoulder.

'You're going to be famous,' he said with that familiar half-smile on his face, 'I couldn't quite work out what it was but you've made everything clear with your drawing.'

Phil and Sonja came over to look but when they saw what I had done they realised they could add no more so they went away again. Satisfied at last I stopped staring down at both photographs and leaned back in the chair. I rubbed my eyes. 'That's better,' I said and leaned forward to check the accuracy of my sketch.

There it was. The new comet.

'Now name it,' said Matt.

Phil and Sonja reappeared close by and also said: 'Yes, now name it.' I thought for a second.

Even if it was me who had made the final breakthrough we were all involved so we should all be part of it. I had not only found the comet I had also tracked its course through the solar-system. It was going very close to the Earth then very close to the sun. It was going to produce the longest tail anyone had ever seen and it was going to be spectacular. I could take all of the credit myself but somehow that wasn't right.

A name.

Smith 1957.

That was the glory name. I couldn't do it.

DMPS 1957. David/Matt/Phil/Sonja 1957. That would include everyone but it was a mouthful. Would it go down in history? Would it be remembered?

Matt had discovered it, or if he hadn't he had put me on the right track. So his name should come first. Phil and Sonja were there as well but who should come first out of them? I couldn't work it out.

I tried again. MDS+P 1957. Matt/David/Sonja and Phil 1957.

That was worse. The discovery had been made, why was naming it so difficult?

I must have tossed and turned in my sleep and I wouldn't have been surprised if I'd shouted as well. The big thing was done, what was the problem with the little thing? There was no easy answer. Their names circulated around my head but to no use. Matt, Sonja, Phil, David. I had discovered it, I should be first. David, David, David. D+SMP 1957. David and the rest. David Smith 1957, forget the others…

'DAVID…'

Yes, alright then, only me…

'DAVID, wake up! It's Saturday morning. You're going Christmas shopping and you're leaving in half an hour. You need a shower and after that, if you've left enough time, breakfast. Wake up and get up NOW!'

I lay stock still in bed. I was sweating and the reason was I had left a dream without finishing it. I hated that feeling. I wouldn't feel right for a long time and there was no going back. You either finished a dream or you didn't.

I groaned and pulled the bedclothes over my head.

I was back in the real world and I didn't like it.

{I may not know what's wrong with him but I do know this: Doing something is better therapy than moping around doing nothing. It will take his mind off things.}

Chapter 21.

Last minute Christmas shopping was my speciality. The previous year it had been Phil and me but this time I was on my own. I sat on the bus and waited with anticipation as it pulled into the new stop outside the observatory. Perhaps Matt would be there and I could find out first-hand what was going on. The bus waited for a few seconds. No Matt. I craned my neck and looked back as the bus moved away but no-one appeared. Reluctantly, I stopped looking.

The bus pulled into its station. Snow was still on the ground but people's feet had turned it into slush and the slush got into my shoes and made my socks wet. My feet turned into blocks of ice. The air was cold and my breath jetted in front of me. Fortunately I had thought to wear a warm coat so my body didn't freeze but every lungful of air cooled me inside. I was afraid of catching pneumonia, this was how you caught it if you believed what old people told you. I already knew I would get chilblains on my feet, they told you that as well. I didn't know what chilblains were but I knew I would be better off not getting them. As I walked away from the bus I remembered what I shouldn't do if I wasn't to make them worse. 'Don't put your feet on top of the fire.' Gran had died five years ago but her voice had stayed with me.

What to buy.

I needed presents for Mum, Dad, Shandy and Phil. And Sonja. These were my personal presents, as Mum had put it, so I had to get them myself. 'Don't worry about Aunts, Uncles, Cousins, I'll get those, you just have to write your name on the cards.' It was a good arrangement.

But what to get.

How much to spend was easy. Four shillings each. Apart from my bus-fare I had a whole pound burning a hole in my trousers. I had put it aside from the years' pocket-money. It was a shame to spend it on other people a voice inside my head said but I quickly told it to be quiet. Mum had explained that buying your presents on your own with your own money was part of growing up and that was all she needed to say. How could I argue with something which proved I was growing up? This logic shut the voice up but I could still hear it grumbling.

Mum and Sonja were easy. A grooming set each. Combs and things. Mum was always combing her hair. I handed over my pound note and happily said yes when the girl asked me if I wanted them wrapped up in Christmas paper. She smiled at me as she handed it over. Her eyes were blue but not like Sonja's. There was something wrong with her smile as well.

Outside the shop I saw the problem immediately so turned my head away and walked past quickly pretending to look at something interesting on the other side of the road. Now I went into a men's shop. Something for Dad. I looked around.

Unfortunately it was one of those shops where someone approaches you and asks if you need any help. 'No,' I said and turned away and before he could say anything else I walked rapidly towards the exit and got out. I didn't like it when that happened. Outside there was the same problem which I again spotted straightaway and so was able to avoid.

Woolworth's. They wouldn't have anyone walking about wanting to annoy me.

I went in. When I came out I had Dad's present. A shaving kit with a new brush. He'd love it. I also had Shandy's: A rubber bone. Now Phil. What to do about Phil. He had most things, his parents had more money than mine and they spent it on holidays, cars, caravans and things for Phil. It would require a special effort but my toes must have frostbite and gangrene by now so the effort would have to be made quickly.

I looked in a few shop windows but nothing stood out and my feet really were beginning to hurt. It had started snowing again so I pulled my hood up over my head and fastened the strap under my chin. Things were getting uncomfortable.

At last. Phil had recently become interested in Airfix models and here in front of me, just in time, was a shop which sold them. I went in. I didn't know which ones he had because he wouldn't show them to me; he said he was still learning how to make them properly and if he showed them to anyone now he would just be embarrassed. I didn't even know what he specialised in. Looking around there were ships, aeroplanes, tanks, even a lighthouse. He wouldn't have one of those, surely. I toyed with the idea but soon noticed there was only one lighthouse. If he had one it would probably be that. On the other hand there were many aeroplanes. I moved over to them and looked at the boxes piled in a heap on top of one another but still in some sort of order. British first, Spitfires and Hurricanes, Wellington and Lancaster Bombers. A Sunderland Flying Boat. That one was a monster, a wingspan like an albatross and hundreds of tiny plastic portholes down its fuselage. Then I looked at the price, neatly stuck on the box, written on a tiny removable sticker. It was more than four shillings.

Underneath were the Germans. Dorniers and Focke-Wulf's, Messerschmitts, a Stuka, Heinkels and Junkers. The Stuka was really a Junker, even I knew that, a Ju-87. I looked at the removable sticker. Eureka. I could go home.

The problem hadn't been there when I had gone into the shop but it was when I wanted to leave. There was no way I could avoid it by looking the other way. So I didn't. I looked straight at the ground and pretended not to hear the rattle of the can and the invitation to buy a flag. It might look rude if you saw me doing this but it wasn't at all. I had worked it all out ages ago. It was the best for both of us.

{I rattled my can for the thousandth time but the boy pretended not to see me and walked past with his head down. It starts early, ignoring people. You get used to it.}

Chapter 22.

My feet warmed up a bit on the way home. I was last off the bus and the driver, alerted by the squelching noises I was making, turned around in his seat to see what it was. He was old. As I got off he warned me about chilblains and I nodded politely.

When I got home I shouted that no-one must come and see me because I had a bag of Christmas presents and that gave me the chance to take off my sodden shoes and go upstairs. I took a towel from the bathroom , sat on my bed and dried my feet.

I wrapped my presents with some difficulty. A big pair of scissors helped. I balanced them on the paper and they weighed down the wrapping until I could sellotape it. That done, I wrote labels and attached them to the presents. I pushed the presents under my bed and went downstairs.

After tea the evening paper arrived. Dad usually fell asleep while he was reading it but this time he found something he thought might interest me. 'Did you know the observatory is having a Christmas party?'

I didn't.

'It's here, look.' He passed the page over to me.

It was a short report on how the staff at Herstmonceux were grateful for everything the local people had done for them since they had arrived and how welcome they'd been made to feel. As a thank-you they were giving a Christmas Eve party to which all were invited. There would be food and drink. All of the resident astronomers would be there to socialise and chat about the work they were involved in. I handed the paper back. I had to see Phil.

'I've just got to out for a bit,' I announced. I heard a groan from the hall. Mum appeared through the lounge door and in her hands she held my shoes.

'I heard that,' she said, 'Not until you do something about these.' My shoes dripped water onto the lounge carpet. Why don't parents ever understand when something is urgent?

Phil's Dad looked surprised when he answered the door but he didn't say anything. He didn't call Phil either, he just said Philip's in his room, go on up.

I listened outside Phil's door. It sounded like he was talking to himself but I couldn't hear clearly enough to understand what he was saying. His voice grew louder and now he appeared to be arguing with himself. Then I heard a swear word. I abandoned my first thought of surprising Phil by abruptly slamming his door open. He really didn't sound in a good mood. Instead I knocked. The swearing suddenly stopped. 'Yes?'

Now how good an impression of his Dad could I do? Not brilliant but Phil wasn't expecting it to be me and his door was shut which would muffle things. I tried not to giggle and said: 'I've never heard such language.'

There was absolute silence from inside the room.

I put on my most severe voice. 'I will not have such words said in this house.' I stuffed my fist into my mouth to stop myself laughing. Now there was a noise from Phil's room. A small noise. I removed my fist for just long enough to demand: 'What was that?'

'I'm sorry.'

'I can't hear you.'

'I said I'm sorry Dad. You weren't supposed to hear it.' My eyes were beginning to water.

'Yes, well you open this door right now and make your apology to me in person like a man.' That was good enough but then I had a flash of inspiration. 'And if you don't I'm going to tell Father Christmas!'

The swearing I had heard before was nothing to the volley Phil let loose now. And my name was included. The door was wrenched open. 'I knew it was you,' Phil insisted. 'No you didn't,' I said happily.

I hadn't been in Phil's room since he caught the Airfix bug. Looking around it was easy to see why none of his models had made it out of his room. There they stood, ships and aeroplanes and a lighthouse all in various states of disrepair. The latest, the one he had been working on and which had provoked the original blast of abuse sat on Phil's desk looking extremely sorry for itself. It took me a moment to decide what it was supposed to be. Definitely some sort of plane but… Phil saw me looking.

'It's a Mosquito,' he said.

There must have been more glue on it than on the real thing. I shook my head. Given that this was the current standard of Phil's ability and remembering there were only two days before Christmas Eve I felt sorry for the model of the Messerschmitt I had bought him. 'Didn't you follow the plans?' I asked.

'I always see a quicker way.'

Phil went over and stood between me and his model. 'Anyhow,' he said, 'What's up? Why are you here?' He folded his arms and waited.

'The observatory are having a Christmas party. There was an invitation in the local paper and it said all the astronomers would be there…'

Phil remained with his arms still folded and didn't say anything. I continued:

'I think we should go. If all the astronomers are going to be there it means Matt will be too. If we can get him on his own we can ask him what's happening, it might be our last chance.' Even Phil would now see the urgency of me coming round to his house and telling him this. I didn't care about his models and him worrying what I thought about them even if he supposed I did. This was something much more important. Phil finally uncrossed his arms.

'I saw that too but I didn't think you'd be interested,' he said.

I felt baffled and I must have given away my feeling by the look on my face.

'Are you sure you want to go?'

I tried to think of a reason why not. Any reason.

'Well, I will if you will but we better get a move on if we're going to go.'

This was cryptic. There was the distinct smell of glue in the room and I wondered if it had somehow affected Phil. Worse, could it have affected me? I had never had a conversation like this with him before, what could he possibly mean? There was no rush, we had no need to hurry, the party was two days away. Why should we have to get a move on?

'Phil…' I began, uncertainly. He started looking in his wardrobe. 'Phil,' I said more firmly and he stopped looking and turned to face me. 'What?'

'We don't need to go right now, you can stop looking for your coat.' It was Phil's turn to appear baffled. 'I wasn't looking for my coat.'

'Then what were you doing in your wardrobe?'

'Looking for something I might be able to adapt into a costume. If I find anything suitable I can start tonight, I've had enough of Mosquito building. I suppose you've already got one to wear. Who are you going as?'

Phil might not be interested in reading aircraft plans but he had read the invitation to the observatory party and he had read it more closely than I had. No wonder he thought I wouldn't be interested. We finally stopped talking at cross-purposes when Phil cleared the air with a simple question.

'You do know it's fancy dress don't you?'

{'Was that Philip swearing?'

'No, I don't think so.'

'Well it sounded to me like it was. I didn't know he knew words like that.'

'He's growing up.'

'Far too quickly. Was that David at the door?'

'Yes.'

'I'm not sure about him. I think he may be a bad influence.'

'Turn the radio up darling, you won't be disturbed then.'

'He's still at it.'

...Shhhh... I'm trying to listen to the radio.'

'... You're not listening to a word I say are you?'}

Chapter 23.

What to go as.

I had two days to think of something and make the costume but so far I wasn't making any progress. The invitation just said fancy dress so that left it wide open but Phil and I decided that a space theme was called for, especially from us. It just wouldn't be right to turn up as Dracula or Frankenstein's Monster, easy though costumes for those would be.

An astronaut was the obvious choice but a silver suit and realistic helmet taxed our inventiveness. We quickly widened our definition of space to include science-fiction books and films. Phil and I were deep in discussion about the books we had read and the films we had seen when Phil's Dad came upstairs to tell me time was getting on and I should leave. Fascinating as our deliberations were he was sure it was nothing which couldn't wait until tomorrow. Phil and I glanced at each-other. How wrong could someone be?

And now here I was with one day to go. I racked my brains and forced myself to think. Half an hour later I had the answer.

The Martians had invaded Earth in War of the Worlds and at the end, when they had lost, the audience caught a glimpse of one of them as its war machine crashed and the pilot tried to crawl out. Although it was only a glimpse that suited me perfectly because then no-one could argue with my costume. Tentacles had appeared on the end of what must have been a hand and the hand had crawled a short way outside the machine. That should be easy enough. Earlier in the film there was a telescopic robot head which had three eyes so if I assumed it had been modelled on the real Martians I could fashion myself a head which looked a bit like it. There wasn't much I could do about my body except cover it in something suitably repellent. Then I realised that if the creatures had three eyes they would probably have three of everything. Three arms, three legs... No, I decided, that was taking things too far.

I went downstairs to the kitchen to see what I could find. Rubber gloves could be worn and the fingers could be made to look like tentacles. A brown paper bag would do for a head with small eye holes cut out so I could see and big spots drawn on the top to stand for the Martian eyes. I had felt-tip pens upstairs. So far so good. In the garage there was an old potato sack which I could wear, its colour was right but the material was too rough to be worn against the skin. These Martians would therefore wear a school shirt underneath and if that wasn't enough, also a vest. I collected everything and went back to my bedroom.

Two hours later I looked at myself in the mirror. The paper bag now looked more convincing with the large amount of cotton-wool I had stuffed up into the top of it. That also gave the effect of a domed head which made the Martians appear intelligent, appropriate I thought for creatures capable of travelling all the way from their planet to Earth. The improvement also gave me more room to make the felt-tip eyes bigger whilst drawing attention away from my own eyes which looked out from holes now significantly further down than half way. I was very pleased with the effect. The rubber gloves were a different matter. They made my hands sweaty but a spot of surgery with a pair of nail scissors across the palms soon solved that. I had remembered we had suckers with coat hooks on which weren't being used so I borrowed several and removed the hooks then sewed the suckers onto the ends of the rubber fingers. Colouring them brown completed the job.

I turned around and looked at myself. Raising my hands I found I could swing the tentacles a bit and if I pulled my fingers slightly out of each glove then made clenching motions could give a good approximation of the movements of the dying Martian. I smiled behind the brown paper bag. I wondered how Phil was getting on.

Five minutes later I knew.

The front door bell rang and I answered it. Phil was standing there with a parcel under his arm. 'I've brought my costume to show you,' he said, 'Have you finished yours yet?' He came up to my room.

'Before you unpack that I'll go first,' I said. I wasn't feeling nearly so confident now it wasn't just me who had to be impressed. I quickly put on the Martian costume.

'Wow,' Phil whistled, 'That's good. Did you make it all yourself?' I assured him I had.

'Ok then. Turn around.' I heard rustling and resisted the temptation to look. After what seemed an age Phil said: 'Ok. I'm ready.'

I turned back. I don't know what I expected but I wasn't prepared for what I saw. Phil had disappeared. He had disappeared inside a body length covering of plastic, polythene to be exact. It completely enveloped him from head to toe.

'How can you breathe inside all that?' I asked anxiously.

'Easily,' he said in a muffled voice, though from his laboured gasping it sounded anything but. I waited, listening to him pant and watched as the part around his face turned even more opaque than it already was.

'Aren't you going to ask me what I am?' he said eventually, his voice sounding even more strained.

'Out of your mind?' I ventured.

Phil tore at the plastic around his head and emerged red-faced and fuming. 'I'm a Pod you idiot, anyone can see that!'

'A Pod,' I repeated.

‘Out of Invasion of the Body Snatchers. The pods were where they grew the replacement humans.’

‘If you stay inside that for much longer you’ll need a replacement for yourself,’ I told him, ‘You’ll suffocate.’

‘No I won’t.’ He started to wrap the polythene around his head again. ‘I’ll prove it,’ said his indistinct voice.

I looked around for my scissors. ‘Hold still,’ I told him but I wasn’t sure he’d heard. I put my mouth close to where I guessed his ear might be. ‘Hold still!’ I cut a hole for him to breathe.

‘Oh, that’s better,’ he said and his voice was now clear. ‘It’s a good costume,’ I told him, ‘But I’m glad you brought it around here first. It might have got embarrassing if you’d passed out at the party.’

Now Phil was out of danger I stepped back and looked at his costume properly. It wasn’t too bad, considering. It was certainly imaginative and more to the point, it looked nothing like mine. I wasn’t sure how well I would take it if a much better Martian than me turned up. In Phil’s case however I doubted if there was enough polythene left in the village to offer him a serious challenge. We were going to be ok. I nodded at Phil and gave him the thumbs-up. He grinned. ‘Of course I wouldn’t have passed out,’ he replied but I could easily detect the note of relief in his voice.

Downstairs, the front-door bell rang again.

Dad answered it and he sounded surprised. Immediately the front door shut he came upstairs and knocked on my door. ‘There’s a telegram for you,’ he said, holding out a small brown envelope. ‘Hope nothing’s wrong. Tell me if there is.’

I had never received a telegram before.

It was from Sonja.

{Karl will kill me if he knows I've sent this. But I had to, it's too important to wait. They'll know what to do, that is they won't but they'll take it to someone who does and then… I hope I get back in time. I know I will. I just know… I have to…}

Chapter 24.

Christmas Eve. Phil and I changed at my house and walked to the observatory. We had to do it that way I explained to Phil. Everybody else would arrive in costume and anyway how did we know there would be anywhere to leave our clothes if we changed when we got there? Also, we wanted to make an immediate impact. Phil reluctantly agreed. It was just as well he did because when he tried to walk out of my bedroom he found he couldn't. My scissors once again provided the solution. We chopped off the final foot of plastic from his pod enabling him to move his feet.

'No-one will look at you below your knees,' I encouraged him, 'Anyway, what were you planning to do? Just lie there in the middle of the floor?'

'The real pods did.'

'It wouldn't be much of a party for you if you did that,' I said.

'But it would be more realistic.'

'Then how am I supposed to get you there? I don't have a flying saucer handy.'

Eventually he saw reason but I could tell he was less than happy.

The newspaper advert and word of mouth had drawn a large crowd and we weren't alone as we walked through the observatory gates. Almost all of the children of the village were dressed up and so, to my amusement, were their parents. It was also obvious that they had taken fancy-dress to mean just that and they hadn't confined themselves to a space theme. Long John Silvers mixed with Hunchbacks of Notre Dame and there were film stars too though I would have had to ask most of them to find out who they thought they were.

Miles Crowner announced loudly that he was 'Elvis Presley' but I hadn't heard of him.

The party was being held in the Nissen hut which served as the recreation room for Junior staff. They had made a big effort to make everyone from the village feel welcome and inside the hut was decorated with a Christmas tree, balloons and tinsel. There was music from a rather battered looking record-player but, being scientists as well as astronomers, the Junior staff had equipped it with a pair of very large home-made loudspeakers which they powered from a car battery. Some of the men from the village who had well-paid jobs had spent a lot of money on equipment supposed to reproduce music as accurately as possible and I saw them gathered around the speakers shaking their heads.

There were two long lines of tables holding plates of food and drink for the children. In one corner was a bar for the adults. Professor Maclachlan checked his watch and on the stroke of seven-thirty the music stopped and he stepped forward to make an announcement. 'Thank you for coming and Happy Christmas!' This got a cheer.

'I have only two announcements. The first is that the domes and the rest of the site are out of bounds. Even though it is Christmas Eve our work continues and as I can see the stars this evening without the aid of a telescope…' he paused for laughter but only his own staff obliged, '…We will certainly be looking at them in closer detail later on tonight. The second announcement is… Please Enjoy Yourselves!'

The music started up again and wrappers were removed from the plates of food. Phil nudged me. 'Dig in.'

'But we have to find him.'

'Work best done on a full stomach.' From nowhere Phil had found two paper plates. He handed one to me and we approached the nearest table.

For someone whose face was mostly covered with plastic Phil didn't waste much time stuffing food into it. I don't know why he bothered with his paper plate, nothing remained on it for any length of time. Across from us were the four from our school who had won the contest to visit the observatory. I noted their costumes, they had attempted to come as aliens from outer space but either their imaginations weren't up to it or they hadn't seen any recent films. I tried not to laugh. Phil also saw them and in-between mouthfuls he did laugh. They saw us and turned away.

The crowd around the bar were growing more noisy. They hadn't had to pay for their drinks so they were making the most of it. Elvis left the bar and approached the record-player and when the current song finished he put a record he had been carrying on the turntable and turned the volume up. Dancing broke out.

Phil and I filled our plates again and went to the side of the room where we sat on the floor.

'No sign of him.'

Phil nodded. 'Perhaps he's banned from coming.'

That was unfair if it was true. I could understand Matt being told off and grounded for letting us use the telescopes but not allowing him to attend the party was taking things too far. After all, it was Christmas Eve. I saw Professor Maclachlan at the bar talking loudly with the people from the village and pulled a face at him. If anyone was, he was responsible for not allowing Matt to be here.

'We'll have to go and find him,' I said to Phil out of the corner of my mouth.

'But where to look.' Phil had polished off yet another sausage roll and was looking hungrily back at the table.

'We have to disobey orders.' I glanced back at Maclachlan. He was enjoying himself so much he wouldn't notice if we slipped out.

'Dressed like this?' Phil said. 'We'll be spotted.'

'No.' I had worked it out. 'How we're dressed is to our advantage. I can say you went outside to go to the toilet but when you didn't come back I went to look for you. If anyone sees us you just say you got lost because you couldn't see properly through that mile of plastic you have wrapped around your head.'

'Mmm. Could work. But the toilets are just over there.'

I had thought of an answer to that as well. 'But no-one told us. The only things we were told were not to go near the domes and to enjoy ourselves.'

'What about that,' said Phil looking at the large sign suspended from the ceiling which read 'Gents' printed above a large arrow pointing towards them.

'We can bluff it,' I assured him, 'What's the matter, are you scared?' That did it. Phil put his plate down.

'Right. Let's go.' He stood up.

I was about to follow him but something caught my eye. Something which left me frozen and sitting stock still on the floor.

'What are you waiting for? Are you scared now?' Phil looked down at me scornfully. I hadn't taken my eyes off what I had seen. Phil hadn't noticed.

'Sit down,' I hissed at him.

'What?'

'Sit down!'

There must have been something in my voice because Phil did sit, sliding himself down the wall and making a scraping sound against it with the plastic covering him.

'What is it?'

'Look.'

At the other end of the room a figure had appeared. It was dressed as yet another science-fiction character and one which I recognised. The bandages around the head gave it away.

'What am I supposed to be looking for?' Phil's voice sounded urgent yet perplexed. He followed my gaze but people had walked in the way and he couldn't see what I had seen. I said: 'Wait until they've gone.'

A few seconds passed. Then the way cleared. 'There. Can you see now? It's the Invisible Man.'

Phil, as usual, took everything literally. 'How can I see the Invisible Man,' he pointed out, 'The whole thing about being invisible is that…' Then he too caught sight of the figure.

'Oh…'

I hadn't been mistaken. Now the bodies had cleared out of the way Phil had a good view of him too. I would have recognised him anywhere.

The Invisible Man was Matt.

{Great disguise! I'm not staying up here all on my own while there's a party going on. Even the Professor will congratulate me on this – I won't be scaring anyone so he can't make a scene and I'll sit by the door so if I don't feel too good I can make a quick exit. Well done me! Maybe I can even replace the bandages before they're noticed missing. There were just enough. Hope no-one needs any before the evening ends. Right – one final look in the mirror to check… Party, here I come!}

Chapter 25.

'Should we go over?' wondered Phil.

I glanced around the whole room quickly. It seemed no-one else had noticed his arrival. The one person most likely to object was Professor Maclachlan and he was having far too good a time drinking at the bar and entertaining the locals. He had no eyes for anything else.

Matt had seated himself at the far end of the table and was sipping at a cup of orange squash. Whether he had got it himself or someone had provided it for him I didn't know but what was clear was that he wasn't talking to anyone nor was anybody bothering with him. The bandages hid his face certainly but surely his colleagues knew who he was. Perhaps they were under orders not to socialise. I looked at him just sitting there and a sudden anger at Professor Maclachlan welled up inside me.

'We have to talk to him.'

'I know.' Phil looked at me. 'Your face has gone red.'

I tried to make it return to its normal colour but my anger hadn't yet subsided. 'We will in a moment,' I said.

'Have you got the telegram with you?'

'Of course.'

I tried to work out how we could approach Matt without getting him into trouble. It was obvious to me that he had sneaked into the party in the best disguise he could think of and that we would be seriously in the wrong if we just went up and started talking to him. If he was found out he would be sent off back to his room completely spoiling his Christmas Eve. Then, no doubt, Maclachlan would find some way of spoiling his Christmas Day and his Boxing Day and his New Year and his entire life. I forced myself to grin and told the blood to drain away from my face and not towards it.

'What's so funny?' asked Phil.

'Nothing.' I kept the fixed grin, baring my teeth in a travesty of a smile. 'This is just in case anyone thinks I'm not having a good time.'

'I'd stop if I were you,' Phil advised, 'You're going to frighten somebody.'

'I'm a Martian remember, intent on destroying all living things on this planet. I'm *supposed* to frighten people. Anyway, listen, I've worked out how we can talk to him.'

Phil and I circled the room but in the opposite direction to where Matt was sitting. We took our time. On the way we acquired another drink each and a fresh paper plate. By the time we reached the far end of the room we knew we weren't being followed and no-one could accuse us of giving away Matt's secret by walking directly towards him. We arrived at the other side of the table to him and Phil and I sat down.

'Have a sausage roll,' I said to Phil in a loud voice.

'Thank you, I will,' answered Phil in equally loud tones. Matt turned his head towards us.

Victory.

'What took you so long,' he said.

{What can I do? I could have him removed I suppose... Did I give him a direct order not to come down here? I'm not sure... No point in making a fuss.

I wonder where his friends are? Oh... I really mustn't laugh but the sight of them creeping around the long way thinking they haven't been noticed is simply too much... I'll pretend I haven't seen them. They must think this is a great adventure. I suppose it is for them and if I were their age I would think so too.

I'll give them time to say hello and then go over to make sure Matt's not being embarrassed by their attentions. I'm not so old I don't remember how children's minds work – they're bound to ask him something personal sooner or later and he may not know what to say. I'll keep an eye on the situation... In the meantime there's no reason why I shouldn't have another drink with my new friends the locals. This party was a very good idea by me – even if I say so myself!}

Chapter 26.

'You can see us,' said Phil.

I looked closely. Matt's bandages didn't cover his eyes completely. So he wasn't quite the Invisible Man.

'Of course,' said Matt, helping himself to a sandwich. ' How do you think I got down here and found myself a chair without help?'

'We thought you were hiding from Professor Maclachlan, that's why we didn't come over straight away.' I tried to explain our manoeuvres. 'We didn't want to give you away.'

'I did wonder. But there was no need. I'm free to roam all I like around here I just can't stay with you anymore.'

Despite what he said I found myself looking at where the Professor was holding court. If he had noticed us talking to Matt he gave no sign.

'So you're under a sort of house arrest,' I said.

Matt chuckled. 'If you like.'

Phil relaxed and congratulated Matt on his costume.

'Mmm. There's a bit more to it than that.' Matt finished his sandwich and poured himself another drink of orange squash. 'But it is a good disguise and at the moment I need one.'

Phil stiffened again and dropped his voice. 'Why? Who are you hiding from if it isn't the Professor?'

Matt lowered his head towards our side of the table before answering. 'It's not me who's hiding from anyone. I'm keeping people from seeing me as I am right now, it might frighten them.'

Phil just stared. A thousand things ran through my mind. What had happened to Matt? What did he mean? Was the observatory a cover for something else? Experiments on humans? Then it made sense that they had moved to a place far from civilisation where such things could be kept quiet. Perhaps it was becoming too hot for them in London and they needed to escape to the middle of nowhere hoping to gain time before they were found out. If the experiments were a success they could move back; if not the evidence could be buried where no-one would think to look. I became nervous. What if the experiment on Matt hadn't been a success? They would also bury anyone who found out the secret or anybody they suspected of finding out. I shivered despite the warmth in the hut. Whether by coincidence or not Professor Maclachlan was now looking directly at me. Could he have guessed I now knew? He seemed to make a strange movement with his hand…

'I'm completely bald,' said Matt.

I jerked my attention back to him. The bandages around his head did seem very tight against his skull and there were no stray hairs visible sticking through the overlapping folds.

'I've been away,' said Matt, 'They're trying to find the cause of my fainting.'

Unseen by me Professor Maclachlan repeated his strange hand movement. It wasn't a secret signal to have me, Phil and Matt removed and taken away it was a secret signal to the astronomer in charge of the record-player to change the song. He'd had enough of 'I'm All Shook Up'.

Matt explained everything calmly. Following the incident with the pool he had been advised to seek the opinion of the local doctor and he'd taken this advice. The village doctor examined him and questioned him about his headaches. That afternoon he went to see a specialist in London who cancelled his appointments for the rest of the day. Before Matt knew what was happening his head was being shaved and a biopsy was being taken.

'There's a real bandage underneath this fake one,' he grinned. Matt wasn't as calm as he tried to appear.

'What's a biopsy?' asked Phil.

'It's an investigation,' said Matt, 'They take a sample and run tests. I'll know the results soon.'

Phil was at his most insensitive. 'What do you think it is?' he asked.

Matt hesitated. 'A number of things…' His voice trailed off. '…None of them pleasant.'

Phil was about to ask Matt to list the unpleasant things, I just knew it. I had to change the subject. Before I did I took the chance to kick Phil hard under the table to tell him to shut up. 'Ouch,' he groaned but I ignored him and quickly said: 'Matt. Sonja sent us a telegram. She had to go to Jodrell Bank with Karl. I think the message she sent is important.' Matt seemed relieved that we were off the subject of his headaches.

'I knew they'd gone up there, Karl was very pleased he'd been invited, he's one of the first outside their Group to be given a chance to see the new radio dish in operation. He'll be full of himself when he gets back.' Matt suddenly became curious. 'And Sonja sent a telegram? What did it say?'

'I'll read it to you.' I took the piece of paper from my pocket and unfolded it.

'It says…'

Phil had recovered from his kick and happened to be looking in the direction of the bar. He didn't like what he saw. 'Watch out. Maclachlan's coming over. He's making a bee-line for us.'

'Perhaps this better wait,' said Matt.

I started to put the telegram away but suddenly the Professor was intercepted. The Fatuous Four had surrounded him and engaged him in conversation. He was still looking over at Matt but he was too polite to push the Four out of his way. That was all the encouragement I needed. I unfolded the telegram again and read it to Matt quickly and urgently.

'Look in Lynx stop. NGC 2419 Stop. On Jodrell's list for next month stop. Won't let Karl investigate until then stop.

Apparently too many interesting things ahead of it stop. Karl is hopping mad stop.'

'What does it mean?' asked Phil.

'Can I see that?' said Matt. I handed it over and he read the message for himself.

'Well?' said Phil impatiently.

Matt shook his head. 'Thirty-five words, must have cost a fortune.'

'Yes, but what do they mean?' Phil's voice was rising. From the corner of my eye I saw Professor Maclachlan finally break free of the attentions of the Four and resume his journey towards us. I looked back at Matt.

'Can you make any sense of it? Is it important?' Matt handed the telegram back.

'Here, you take it. I'll remember what it says, it's plain enough. I don't want to be caught with it though, Sonja will be in enough trouble with Karl when he finds out she's sent it and the last thing I need now is to be on the end of his temper.'

I folded the telegram back into my pocket just as Professor Maclachlan arrived. He stood over us and looked down at Matt.

'I'm pleased to see you're feeling well enough to come to the party Matthew; I take it these children aren't bothering you?'

I sensed Phil's hackles rising and gave him another kick.

Matt smiled at the Professor's insensitivity. 'No, everything's fine. These amateur astronomers are keeping me company, they aren't causing any trouble.'

Professor Maclachlan looked more closely and appeared to recognize us. 'Oh, I see. They're the ones who were with you when…'

Matt nodded. 'That's right.'

'Well… We've spoken about that haven't we? You know not to take them into the domes any more…' He hesitated and it seemed as if he didn't want to hurt either our or Matt's feelings. I could sense him groping for the right words to say. Eventually he managed: 'Even though it's a very good thing they're interested in astronomy.'

'It is Professor. And don't worry, I won't be doing anything unsupervised until the results are known.'

He looked surprised. I knew the Professor wanted to ask Matt if he had told us about his situation. Perhaps he would later. Just then we, and he, were saved by a commotion at the bar. 'I'd better be going,' the Professor said, 'The locals want to say goodbye.'

I looked over to where Miles Crowner and his friends were beckoning the Professor back for a final drink before the free bar closed. They wanted to express their gratitude and they weren't going to take no for an answer. Matt watched him go and nodded thoughtfully.

'Are you thinking about the telegram?' asked Phil.

'Sort of,' said Matt. Then he turned his attention back to us. 'Do you want to know what it means?'

No-one else was in earshot. The party was winding down and people were preparing to leave. We would never have a better chance.

Matt lowered his voice. 'It might be important or it could be nothing.'

The final drinks had been swallowed in a hurry at the bar and Professor Maclachlan was receiving many claps on his shoulders and thumps on his back. He had never been so popular. Matt spoke quickly.

'Lynx is a constellation, not a well-known one, not one that you can easily see without a telescope. A man called Johannes Hevelius invented it in the seventeenth century and the story goes that he named it because you would need the eyes of a Lynx to see it as it was so faint. He was much more interesting than any modern astronomer. He was a lawyer, he became

Mayor of Danzig and he was a member of the Beer Brewer's Guild. In fact he was so good at brewing he became leader of the Guild. People did many things with their lives in those days.' Matt stopped and for a moment it seemed as if he was back with Johannes and his pints of beer all those years ago.

'Yes,' said Phil, totally caught up in all of this, 'My Dad says that people nowadays don't do nearly so many things as they should because all their creative time is taken up watching other people do stupid things on television.'

Matt smiled but I knew he was still with Johannes. I waited a second then prompted: 'What else?'

'He'd have been right at home over there at the bar,' mused Matt, which was no answer. Finally he remembered himself.

'NGC 2419. NGC are the initials of the New General Catalogue. That's a list of interesting objects in the sky. It's quite old as it happens but still useful. 2419 is particularly interesting, though I wouldn't have thought it was worth a look now, it's well known.'

'Why?' I asked.

'It's the Intergalactic Wanderer.'

'What's that?'

'A globular cluster of stars that looks like it's escaped from the Milky Way, if it was ever a part of it. It's so far away it counts as being between galaxies. The view back to us must be amazing.'

The bar had closed.

'Karl has found something there,' I said suddenly.

'So it seems,' said Matt and from his voice I could tell he was smiling. 'They must have let him loose with the big dish for a while. But Karl being Karl he probably demanded everyone drop everything and indulge him. Judging by that telegram they refused.'

It was almost time to go.

'Will you look?'

‘I’m not supposed to go anywhere near the telescopes until I’m given the all clear,’ said Matt, ‘So I guess I’d better not.’

Then it really was time to go.

I looked back to wave to Matt as Phil and I reached the door but he had vanished. But I knew he was going to look, he wouldn’t be able to resist it. He was probably on his way up to the domes right now.

{Lynx, Karl Olsson. Lynx is it? Now what could you have found there???

I suppose you demanded to use the dish and to humour you they pointed it at something which wouldn’t cause any trouble. Except you found something interesting, or you claimed to. I suppose Sonja has it right… Yes, I trust her, but do I trust you? Perhaps you’re just playing a game and putting us all on the wrong track.

The Wanderer. It’s so well known. Our records moved here with us, it’s going to be easy to compare them, it won’t take more than five minutes of observation. I can feel another headache coming on, probably as a result of the bright lights and the excitement of the party not to mention the noise. But if there’s anything in the visible to match what you claim to have seen in the radio the Yapp will spot it. And I can scoop you!

I’ll go and take a look. It can’t hurt.}

Chapter 27.

For the first time ever Christmas Day was an anti-climax. I compared it to those in the past and tried to feel the same excitement but couldn't.

Mum and Dad knew there was something wrong when I didn't wake up before them. They seemed pleased about their lie-in though. I dutifully said thank-you for my presents but my heart wasn't in it.

The morning passed in a haze.

Christmas lunch was served, we listened to the Queen, Dad fell asleep; it started to snow. I went outside without enthusiasm and started to make a snowman. Then it got dark. I came back inside and went up to my room. It continued to snow.

Boxing Day brought no let up. I mooned around the house and garden, lost.

The day after that Phil called round. 'Thanks for the Messerschmitt,' were his first words as he stood at the door. 'I followed the plans this time, it doesn't look too bad.'

We sat in my room looking out over the snow filled street and the fields in the distance. We were both thinking exactly the same thing but neither of us wanted to be the first to talk about it. There had been no further contact from Sonja and certainly nothing from the observatory. Short of going up there and asking we couldn't think how we would find out what if anything was happening and we didn't dare do that. What sort of welcome would we get? Eventually we did talk but we just went round in the same old circles. It was not knowing that was the problem.

Another day slipped by.

Then it was New Year's Eve.

I remember feeling abandoned. That was silly and selfish but I couldn't help how I felt. There was no further word from

Sonja, I could only assume she had run out of money or Karl had caught her trying to send another telegram and put a stop to it furious because she was giving away his secrets. Or maybe she just assumed we had it all under control down here and wonderful things awaited her arrival. In that case she thought too much of us. I was in the garden throwing snowballs when this gloomy notion occurred. I threw one particularly fiercely to derail my train of thought.

And Matt. Had he abandoned us too?

The snowman had a name. It was the ugliest snowman with the remains of snowballs suck all over it, making it look as if it had boils all over its face and body. Some boils were growing on top of other boils but there was still room. I made another snowball and threw it, hard. Professor Maclachlan didn't look like that in real life but I had read The Picture of Dorian Gray and I knew he was like that inside.

And then Mum appeared and she was waving at me, beckoning me towards her urgently. She was shouting something as well, something about the observatory and a telephone call for me. I dropped my latest snowball and ran as fast as I could.

Phil and I were sitting in the waiting room outside Professor Maclachlan's office. The phone call had been from him asking if I could go as soon as possible up to the observatory. He had something important he wanted to tell me. He also said to bring 'that other boy, I'm sorry I don't know his name.' He wouldn't tell Mum what it about. As I left she said she hoped everything was alright. The door opened and Professor Maclachlan stood there and when I looked at his face I saw sadness and helplessness and I knew everything was far from alright.

'Come in,' he said.

We sat in two chairs facing him like two naughty schoolboys.

'There is no easy way to tell you this…' he began.

And stopped. He looked down at a piece of paper he was holding then scratched the side of his face and rubbed his hand under his chin. He hadn't shaved.

'Earlier this morning I received a telephone call from St. Bartholomew's Hospital in London. I don't know if you've heard of it?'

We shook our heads. He smiled wanly.

'It's not important. I'm afraid there is bad news. Matthew Day… Matt… was a patient there undergoing tests and two days ago they found something. It was the cause of his headaches…'

'Looking through telescopes was the cause,' said Phil suddenly, 'I know because I saw him rubbing his eyes after he'd been observing. What have they found out? Does it mean he can't be an astronomer anymore?'

I had tried telepathy with Phil once before and knew it didn't work. How could I tell him he was wrong? Then I remembered where I had last seen a grown-up with the same look on his face as the Professor's when he opened his door. I knew what was coming next. Professor Maclachlan tried to break it gently.

'It was discovered too late… There was a deep-seated tumour behind an eye… It was impossible to operate. Matt died this morning… Even if they'd known about it weeks ago the outlook wasn't good. There was nothing anyone could have done…'

'No,' whispered Phil. 'People that young don't die.'

'I'm sorry,' said Professor Maclachlan.

'It was good of you to tell us,' I found myself saying, stiffly.

'I think he would have wanted me to, he was a friend of yours after all.' The Professor seemed relieved that he'd got the awkwardness out of the way and appeared keen to move on. He shuffled papers on his desk. 'Now, there's something else.'

He picked up the sheet he had been holding. 'Matt left you a message. It's addressed to all three of you but of course Sonja isn't back yet from Manchester. I have no idea what it means but apparently Matt was most insistent it be passed on so I'm going to read it to you.'

I glanced over at Phil but he didn't respond. Professor Maclachlan cleared his throat.

'I followed up what you told me and it is something reasonably interesting. I would have liked to have shown you it myself but everything's on the blink, so never mind. When I get out of here we'll get together again. Bring soup and sandwiches! Regards, Matt.'

The Professor put the note down.

'I don't suppose that means anything to you?' he asked.

'He promised us a comet,' I said, quickly. 'Perhaps he found one.'

'A comet,' repeated the Professor and smiled. 'That would have been something. You get to name it you know.'

Phil and I left. Half way down the drive to the observatory Phil said: 'But Sonja's telegram didn't mention anything about a comet.'

'I know,' I replied. 'But I wasn't going to say that to him.'

{A comet. Oh well. Let someone else get a feather in their cap, though it would be a fitting memorial if there really was one and it could be named for Matt. But it's not important enough to interrupt the work of the observatory for something so mundane. On the other hand… Perhaps he didn't mean what I took him to mean. Maybe it's not him who's on the blink but the Yapp. Nobody has been up there to check since he fell ill. Where's my notepad? I must leave a memo for maintenance. I hope he hasn't damaged anything, it will cost a fortune to fix.}

Chapter 28.

Sonja found it hard to believe.

'I wasn't gone that long,' she said.

'Long enough,' said Phil. 'Were you at Jodrell Bank all the time?'

'We left the day after I sent the telegram. They wouldn't let Karl do what he wanted so we visited friends. They did offer to let Karl sit in on their programme of observation but he said we had to leave. I think he was sulking.'

Phil and I digested this. 'When did you find out?' I asked.

'As soon as we returned.'

We told Sonja about the party and the effect her telegram had on Matt. 'He went up to the telescope to check if it was important but it must have been the last thing he did as an astronomer. He had to have realised something was not right with himself because he went straight from here to hospital and he never came back. His note to us must have been written there.'

'Do you have the note?' Sonja asked.

Phil and I shook our heads. The Professor hadn't let us see it much less let us keep it.

'Perhaps it also contained private stuff. Perhaps Matt knew he might not make it and wrote other things that we shouldn't see.'

'Whatever it was we'll never know,' said Phil sadly. 'I wonder if he had any family?'

We thought for a moment.

'He never mentioned any,' I said finally, 'Or if he did I don't remember. He couldn't have been married.'

'No,' agreed Phil. 'Otherwise you'd have had to put up Mrs. Matt as well. I don't suppose he ever mentioned her?'

'He couldn't have been married,' declared Sonja. 'Any wife would demand he gave up observing at night and went to bed at a sensible time.'

Phil snorted. 'How can you observe if not at night? That's when the stars are out!'

Sonja looked at him pityingly. 'The stars are out during the day as well, in fact they're always 'out'. It's just that sunlight swamps them. Where I've been observation can be carried out at any time of day. Radio telescopes aren't affected by sunlight.'

'You're saying if Matt got married he would have to retrain?' demanded Phil. 'He'd only just started working with the telescopes here, he was really excited with what he was doing, he wouldn't give it all up just to get married!'

'His wife would make him,' countered Sonja.

'Then he's married the wrong one,' answered Phil hotly, 'Matt wouldn't do that, he'd marry someone who didn't mind what he did, someone who encouraged him, someone who understood!'

I thought Sonja would carry on with the argument but to my surprise she didn't. Instead she said: 'There's no point in continuing this, it's all conjecture anyway and you don't really know what you're talking about. Now. Do you think Matt discovered something?'

Phil's eyes grew wide. 'You've only just found out he's dead! Shouldn't you mourn a bit more? Instead of trying to become famous on the back of his work?

'There's no point in me mourning, I didn't know him all *that* well. I'm sorry it happened of course…'

Phil had had enough. He turned his back on Sonja.

'… But science goes on. It's bigger than one individual.'

I shook my head. Perhaps this was really Karl's influence and Sonja was too young to know better. She would improve, given time, I was sure of it.

'Well?' She was waiting for an answer.

Phil refused to look at her never mind anything else.

'We don't know, we're guessing,' I said. 'His note just said he had found something interesting but it didn't say what it was. Then it said he would show it to us but the equipment was faulty so he couldn't. He promised he would when he was better but that will never happen now.'

Sonja sat and thought for a second. 'That doesn't make sense,' she said.'

'It's what the note said,' I answered, surprised. 'I'm certain. Phil was there as well.'

'Yes, he's right,' said Phil, 'That's what Maclachlan read out to us.' Phil had turned around now and was looking at Sonja with distaste.

'But it just doesn't make sense,' she persisted. 'How can he discover something if the instruments he is using are broken?'

'For someone so clever you can be dim sometimes,' Phil told her. He didn't elaborate further, he just left the words hanging there.

'Then you explain it.'

'It could be any number of things.' Phil was trying not to rise to her bait. I could see him controlling his voice and making every effort to remain calm.

'Go on then.'

He was wasting his time of course. Sonja could outstubborn a cat.

'Alright. Suppose he did find something but then the telescope went kaput. That would explain his message. Or suppose the telescope is fine but whatever it was he used to record the information malfunctioned, that would explain it too. Or perhaps nothing's wrong with any of the equipment it was just his eyes letting him down again so he said *he* was on the blink. That's just the sort of thing he would say, it's his sense of humour.'

Sonja didn't seem impressed. She looked like she was turning things over in her mind.

'What was that phrase again? I am not familiar with it. On the...?'

'Blink,' I said, completing her question. 'It's what you say when something isn't working – when something's broken.'

'On the blink,' Sonja repeated.

'That's right.'

'Are you sure that was exactly what Matt's note said?'

'Of course I'm sure. Phil heard it too, that was the exact phrase.'

Sonja smiled slowly.

'I think Matt was being clever.'

'What's clever about breaking equipment?' Phil asked on the verge of exasperation. 'There's nothing smart about that it just means...'

Sonja's smile broadened. 'Too clever for you,' she said enigmatically.

'I give up.' Phil rose. 'I'm leaving, I'll see you tomorrow.' His comment was directed to me and very obviously did not include Sonja.

'If you go now you'll miss all the fun.'

Phil turned towards Sonja. 'What did you say?'

'It's a good job I came back. You two are hopeless.'

In spite of himself Phil laughed. What Sonja said next stopped him dead.

'Don't you get it? Matt didn't mean anything was broken at all he just wanted to hide it from the Professor. He wanted us to share his discovery. Presumably because we put him on the right track. 'On the blink' doesn't mean what you think it means. He's telling us the discovery is On The Blink. He means it's on the Blink Comparator!'

Chapter 29.

Sixty years later I can remember what happened next as if it were yesterday.

We waited until it was midnight then went up to the domes. There was no-one guarding them and we weren't seen. Professor Maclachlan hadn't yet assigned anyone to the Yapp in Matt's place presumably because he still thought the equipment was out of order. The door to the dome was unlocked and we went in.

Sonja operated the blink comparator. She had been right. The evidence of Matt's discovery was right there, right in front of our eyes.

We didn't dare tell anyone at Herstmonceux. For all we knew they would cover it up or claim the glory for themselves and we couldn't have that, Matt would never have forgiven us.

So the next day Phil and I rang The Times in London. We probably didn't make much sense but we stirred enough interest for a reporter to be dispatched to the observatory. That same morning Sonja had told Karl everything and he had enough clout to insist on seeing for himself what we had seen. He and the Professor met the reporters. The rest is history.

Now I stood in a small graveyard outside the village.

Further back, hidden, were television cameras feeding into large vans with huge satellite dishes on their roofs ready to bounce pictures of what was about to occur all over the planet. I stood, calmly, waiting. I had watched similar scenes myself on the TV but had never been present live, as it were. Sonja stood beside me, or should I say Professor Sonja Sorenson stood beside me. Even when it had become clear all those years ago what we had discovered and what it meant she had opted to continue with her ambition to become a scientist and she had succeeded. She had Kept The Faith. Many hadn't, Phil amongst them. After a short life of dissipation he had died many years ago. I stood and shivered slightly though it wasn't cold. I hoped Phil had enjoyed himself and had no regrets about what we had done. I had none.

When we looked through the blink comparator and saw the new dot moving from side to side we didn't know what we had found. Phil said it was the comet Matt had promised us, I thought it must be a new planet further out than Pluto. Sonja didn't guess or if she did she never told us. She simply went to the one person who knew enough to be certain.

Later we learned it was an accident, a million to one chance. They had been on their way having detected us but they didn't want us to wait too long before they got here for fear we would become unstable so they were maintaining their equivalent of radio silence. An error on their ship sent a burst of radiation towards the Earth and though it was detected and stopped very quickly the nature of their faster than light communication meant that the burst was spread over several days. Karl detected it at Jodrell Bank and it was still there when Matt went looking. They needn't have worried. We did go a little unstable for a time I suppose but we got over it. In fact, although they didn't know, they did us an enormous favour. The cold war stopped immediately as did other skirmishes scattered around the globe and for very good reason. People expecting guests put their house in order.

Once they knew their secret was out they dropped all pretence. They made contact and kept it up all the way here. They started with medical advances: No-one has died of cancer since 1958. They showed us new ways of generating electricity: We haven't had to burn coal or oil since 1960. Then they proved that all of our religions were wrong and it was as if the world breathed a collective sigh of relief and grew up overnight.

But they kept their biggest surprise until they arrived.

It was beginning. A shape was forming.

They could resurrect the dead.

They started with the most famous. Einstein took it in his stride and appeared most amused to be proved wrong. Newton never did quite get over it.

Then they resurrected political leaders, probably because they hadn't worked us out yet and thought we might need reassurance but times had changed. If it proved anything it only proved that such men were products of their own time and circumstance. When that was removed they didn't seem so impressive though I do remember the rather forced smile on President Kennedy's face when he was invited to shake hands with Lee Harvey Oswald.

Then it was time for a minor ceremony in a small village in Sussex. It is important that the story be complete, they had explained, for us as well as for you.

Sonja grasped my hand. The shape was almost solid and it had its back to us. I would have recognised him anywhere.

Matt was facing them because they wanted him to see them first, that way they said they could explain what had happened and he wouldn't go into shock. I wonder if that was the truth or if they were just heightening the dramatic tension. It isn't every day the discoverer of life elsewhere in the Universe comes face to face with his discovery then turns around to greet the people who had helped him. I looked at Sonja. She was unrecognisable from the girl Matt had known in 1957. And I didn't need a mirror to tell me how much I had changed. What if he didn't recognise us?

Matt was one of the lucky ones. I remember the outcry when they said they weren't going to resurrect everyone who had died. Then, the next day, they said they would arrange it so that if a living person thought of somebody deceased and linked that memory to a specific event they would hear inside their head the thoughts of that person as if they were alive and talking to them face to face. I had no idea how that could possibly work nor what the consequences of it would be. But it was too late to worry about it now.

Matt was turning around and Sonja squeezed my hand ever so hard.

I was going to greet him by name and tell him who we were. I was going to smile and welcome him back. I was going to look him in the eye and tell him thank you for what he had done for us that night long ago. Then I was going to ask him if he thought we had done the right thing.

I wonder what he'll say?

Printed in Great Britain
by Amazon